DRAKEN

THE DRAGLEN BROTHERS SERIES

*Donated in
Milo Folley's honor
By Solease M Barner*

By Solease M Barner

Paradox
Publishing
Covers & Formatting
http://paradoxbooktrailerproductions.blogspot.com.au

Copyright © 2013 by Solease M Barner

ISBN-13: 978-1492843856

ISBN-10: 1492843857

Editing: Tabitha Ormiston-Smith

THANK YOU

I have to thank all my readers, who support me in my writing. I appreciate all the thoughtful things you do to share my book with others. I feel very blessed when I encounter many of you on my website, Facebook, emails, and even in public. I hope to encounter more of you in the future.

I hope you enjoy the new series, readers! ☺

I must thank a few people individually, Jane A. Bowen. Jane, you are a special woman. I love how you take the time to do sweet things that help promote my books. I love my special banner you created! I thank you from the bottom of my heart and I hope you enjoy the new series!

Denise Bush take a bow, you go far and above what is required. The love you pour out to all authors is amazing. Thank you for supporting me, and for letting me grace your FB cover among so many great other authors. Thanks for the gifts you make for my books, they are special to me. I'm happy you enjoy my books, and hope you enjoy this new series!

Diana B. Tan, thank you for always retweeting my books on Twitter. I'm not experienced on twitter, I'm truly grateful for any help I get. I thank you for supporting my work, sharing and always coming to party with me!

There are so many of you who go out of your way for me, I can't name you all, but know I love you all! I look forward to getting feedback on this series from you all! ☺

The Special People working on the book to make it perfect.

Tabitha Ormiston-Smith, you know how to make a girl work. You are the best editor I've encountered. I love you when the book is complete, and think you are an evil witch during editing lol ☺ I know I can say that to you. I always say to myself, Tabitha and I are in a love/hate relationship. I know when you are angry when I see caps in comments on edits. I also know when something made you giggle as well. I appreciate you teaching me to be better at writing, and keeping my feet to the fire. I love working with you and look forward to more books together!

Patti Roberts, you are full of talent! I look forward to doing covers with you. The way you bring life to my vision on a cover is amazing. I'm like a kid in a candy store when I know we are working on covers. You're always so patient with me, very accommodating, and kind. ☺ I always say you're heaven sent and I mean that. I can't wait to work with you, it's such joy to spend time working on covers with you, even when I ask for changes after I've said 'I love it', you change it without complaint, and for that I thank you deep down.

Beta Readers

I LOVE YOU ALL!! I truly enjoy how you are all so truthful with me about my books. I won't give names, because I like to keep my beta readers to myself! ☺ You all know who you are, my first readers. I always look forward to your feedback. You are all awesome!

SPECIAL THANKS

I'm not ashamed and will always thank my heavenly father Jesus Christ. I would not even be here without Him. I have to thank my wonderful husband. I'm so blessed to share my life with you. I love that you are so accepting of my madness, when writing, editing, promoting, and the crazy schedule I have, still you never complain. To my precious daughter, Mommy loves our time together. I love that smile and how we can talk about anything. You will always be my baby. Thank you Mom and Dad, for supporting me with all the wisdom you give me. I love you both, and consider it a blessing to have you as parents. I love all my sisters and love each one of you for being there for me no matter what. Shatina, my manager, I love you so much; you always make sure I stay focused, reminding me of all the important things, and pushing out the negative. Thank you. To my nephew/son, I love talking with you. You are so wise at such a young age, your advice is appreciated. To my friend who is awesome, I love reading books with you and discussing our fictional boyfriends, you know who you are, SWH!!! LOL. To the best book club ever, I love all of you and enjoy our meetings, with such great food and wine! If I have missed anyone please don't charge it to my heart. I love all my family and friends!

Solease M Barner

PURPLE REIGN!

You were not planned

You invaded my life

You changed me

You caused me pain

You even lied to me

Yet, here I stand

Loving You

Wanting You

Needing You

Caressing You

Now, when it's my time to

Reign,

We both shall wear the crown,

Called the

Purple Reign!

By Solease M Barner

CESS

BOOM! Bang, bang, BOOM, is the sound I hear first thing in the morning. The new neighbors are moving in two houses down, and I can hear all their noise as I try to sleep. It's Saturday and my day off from work and school. It's my senior year in college, and I'm still at home with my parents. I decided to go local rather than leave the nest. I love my home, and I want to save money to take my dream trip after I graduate, to beautiful historic Italy, without any help from my parents. I have always wanted to go, enjoying the people and the history. That's why it's so important for me to get my rest, as midterms are coming. I must continue with my GPA of 3.8 if I want the gift my parents promised, which is my very own first place, with them paying the first six months rent. I drag myself out of bed and stumble over to the window to see why all the noise. Glancing at the clock, I notice it's only 8:00 a.m. I wouldn't normally be out of bed until at least 11:00 a.m. My parents are gone for the weekend, and D, who is my twin brother and best friend, will sleep until noon. Nothing will wake him, not even if the house was on fire. I look out the window harder, to see if the neighbors are visible. I only see that it's four men carrying boxes. I grab my binoculars to get a better look. I focus and see a man giving orders. I can't see his face, as his back is to me. I try to focus on the others, but they are behind the moving truck. I feel like Mrs. Peters, the Nosey Parker. I crawl back into bed and try to go back to sleep, but my chance has passed, and I decide to have breakfast. I usually have a yogurt and some toast, but today I'll eat a man's breakfast. I start making pancakes, eggs, sausage, toast, and hash casserole. If I'm going to be up, I might as well eat good food. I could have asked Gloria (she is our live - in maid, plus she cooks better than the cook) to prepare the meal, but I like cooking for myself sometimes. It's not long before my twin brother smells the food, and comes into the kitchen sniffing.

"Cess, I know you made enough for me? I was out late with the guys, and I'm starving," he says, grabbing himself a sausage right out of the pan.

"Hey, I'm not sure if they are done." I smile.

"Doesn't matter to me, if I die from one small half-done sausage then I guess it was my time," D says, grabbing the orange

2

juice. He pours himself a big glass, and proceeds to tell me about his wild night out. His story is interrupted by loud laughter outside.

"Who the hell is laughing like that?" D says, shaking his head. I frown at him, because D can be extremely loud sometimes. The laughter is loud, and the houses are not that close together in this area.

"That might be our neighbors . . . let me go see," I say, walking into the front room. The laughter gets louder. I peek out the window and it's those guys who just moved in. Now that I'm fully awake, I can see them clearly. It's four of them, and they look amazing. They are all over 6 feet, closer to 6'6" then 6'4". My mouth is open when D comes and interrupts my fantasy.

"Cess, you are not ready to be in another relationship, you just broke up with Travis," he mumbles through toast and sausage.

"Look D, I'm over Travis. I thought we agreed not to mention his name in this house," I say, as I turn to finish gazing at these fine men. There is nothing wrong with looking, but I will not break my promise. No men until I'm done with school and have started my career. They can be such a distraction, and looking at these guys, they could be a huge distraction. I will stay away from them.

"Cess, I know that look, stay away from them. I can't go through another boyfriend with you," D says, leaving the room.

I yell back, "I have only had two boyfriends, D!" I think how torn up I was when Travis and I ended our relationship. I'm pretty sure I didn't eat for a week. Maybe I should be nice and introduce myself to the new neighbors.

"D, I think after I eat I'm going to go meet the new neighbors," I say, making my way back to the kitchen.

"Umm . . . Cess, remember your promise?" D mumbled.

"I'm just going to say hi, that's all," I say.

I finish my food and head upstairs for a quick shower. I put on a pair of short shorts and a tank, and walk out the door. The closer I get, the more I realize I haven't talked with a guy (outside of D and his friends) since Travis. What was I thinking, coming out here? I should just turn around. Yep, that's what I'm going to do. As I turn, I hear a very deep voice call out.

"Hey . . . hey you, are you going to come introduce yourself, or are you going to go home?" The voice is friendly. I had thought they were talking and hadn't seen me. I turn slowly, and he is right there.

"Ah . . . hi," I say, looking at this man. He is beautiful. He has long blond hair that's all wet from working out in the sun. His body is perfect. His eyes are amazing, deep green, and he's smiling at me, and those dimples! Yikes, I'm in trouble.

"Hello, I'm Showken, and you are?" he says, with his hand out. Feeling embarrassed, I realize my face is red from looking at his beauty.

"I . . . I'm Cess" I say, shaking his hand.

"Hello Cess, I told my brothers you were nice and I would come introduce myself," he says, with the kind of deep voice that should only be heard in private.

"Umm . . . yeah, how do you say your name again? I'm sorry," I say, feeling really rude. I have never heard of a name like that before.

"Showken, like Show and Ken put together." Showken smiles as he says it again. I notice he is still holding my hand, as two more of them walk up. I'm not going to make it. I have a promise to keep, no men and especially no sex. I'm staying focused on my studies and my career.

"Brother, what have we here?" One of them has short, dark brown hair. His body is huge and he smells so good. He has amazing light gray eyes. He only has on some cut-off shorts, sandals, and a amazing chest that's illegal, or it should be. I can't wait to tell my girlfriends about the new neighbors.

"This is Cess, Cess meet my brother Gemi. The one who is just looking is shy, and that's Layern," Showken says, smiling at me.

"So Cess, are you going to come over?" Gemi says, narrowing his eyes as if he is searching for something.

"I should be heading home. I, umm..." I can feel all their eyes intensely on me. Layern's eyes are really blue, and he is quiet, but just as handsome. The other two are not shy at all. They are all smiles. I bet these brothers are fun. No, I can't think like that, I must remember my studies and career.

"Come on, Cess, we never have company," Showken says,

pulling me towards their home. I feel my feet moving, and turning, I see the other two behind me. I should be afraid to be walking with these guys, they are strangers, but I feel no fear at all. As we make our way to the lawn, the door opens. I see him, and his stare is cold. He has long, jet-black hair, which is pulled into a neat ponytail hanging down his back. There is no smile on his face at all, just a cold look. I feel his eyes roam my body, and now I feel uncomfortable. I guess he's not the friendly brother.

"Brothers, why is she here?" He speaks as though I'm not standing there. I feel insulted and a little humiliated. This man cuts Showken off before he can speak, and marches right up to me, looking down at me as if I am nothing.

"Look, stay off my lawn. Go! Now!" he snarls.

Showken speaks up for me, "Draken, she's okay, ask Layern," he says, as he comes and stands beside me. I'm not afraid of him. I may be smaller, but he will not talk to me like that.

"Draken . . . is that how you say it? Well, you are rude, and I was invited, so don't snap at me," I say, seeing his light purple eyes glaring at me. His brothers move away from me, going inside the house one by one.

"Cess, I will take your tone as a sign of ignorance. You stay off MY lawn, and you will remain intact," Draken says, as he grabs my arm, walking me off the lawn, past his property line and into the street. I've never been treated like this by a guy in my life. He is the rudest man I have ever met, although he looks so hot with those eyes, that hair, and that smooth tan skin. I try to pull away, but he is so strong. My face is turning red, how humiliating is this?

"Let go of me," I snap. He releases me as soon as I'm in the street feeling like trash.

"Cess, be a good neighbor and mind your business, and stay off the property. This is your warning, next time I will ask something of you," Draken says, turning and walking away. I can't help but notice how perfect his walk is. And as the wind blows, I catch his smell, and I know that, though he is as mean as anything, Draken could make me give up my promise.

"Draken, if you ever put your hands on me like that again, I will give you a kick that will make having babies a problem," I say. He stops and looks over his shoulder, continuing to walk towards the house.

I stand there for a second before I make the short, but embarrassing, walk home. I turn and look back, and see the other brothers working, not saying anything now. Draken is outside watching. He turns and looks at me. We stare for a long time, and I finally break the staring contest and head back inside. I lean back against my door, and see his beautiful eyes in my head.

"Draken," I say out loud. Good thing I made the promise of no men, just finishing college and going to Italy before starting my career.

DRAKEN

I'm glad it's only six months this time. We are here for business only. The corporation needs to hire new management, as profits have gone down. I will not tolerant incompetence in our business. Every time we have to check on the businesses, no matter what state we are in, Showken always finds a girl for his pleasure. Well, not this time, I'm not having it, or I will send him back home. There are plenty to play with there. I just had to march some little girl off the lawn, on our first day, because Showken can't keep his smile to himself. We must discuss this.

"Showken, no girls on the property, at the office, or in the car at all. Leave them alone," I growl. That girl, Cess, is going to be a problem, I can tell.

"Draken, listen, just because you have this 'no play while working' doesn't mean I have to follow. I like females and they like me, just relax, I never harm them," Showken says, calmly.

"Six months and we are home, away from this place. Keep it in your pants, or I might ask you for something, just do as I ask," I snap. We have finished the unloading, and Layern and Gemi are setting up downstairs in the basement.

"Okay, Draken, I will honor your request," Showken smirks. I know my brother and I are going to have trouble, since that Cess just had to come down the street with those extremely too-short shorts. Although her legs are beautiful and strong, like a dancer's, and that beautiful brown hair does not help matters, she is a nuisance. I could really make her scream out. I'm nothing like my brother. I have plenty of women waiting to pleasure me when I get home. I have self-control.

"Draken, what are you thinking?" Layern asks, narrowing his eyes, Layern and his gift. Whatever you have got hidden in your mind or heart, Layern knows how to find it.

"I'm just thinking about the interviews coming up this week," I say, trying to push it way down, so he can't see it, but my brother's perceptions are too fast.

"I could have sworn I saw you thinking about Cess, you know, the neighbor you were so rude to, and whose legs you were looking at," Layern says with one brow up. Shit, what am I going to say? She is attractive, and she did make me want her, even with her threats? That little girl has to stay away from me.

"Oh, so that's why she had to leave, you want her. Brother, all you had to do was say something, and I would have backed off," Showken frowns.

"I don't want that girl, and Layern, stay out of my head," I say, done with the discussion. I return to my office and start working on new layouts for the office here in Arizona. I hear Showken yelling through the closed door: "Draken, if you want her, just say it." I totally ignore my favorite brother. I love all my brothers and sisters, but Showken is the only brother I never fought with, growing up. I often experienced jealousy from my siblings for being the oldest, and heir to the throne. I had the misfortune to be born first, and now I have all these expectations, not only from our parents, but all our kind as well. Showken treats me just like a normal brother. I fight with some of my other brothers, and blood has been shed more than once. When I got word that we had to visit Earth, I was displeased. I love living in Kalin, the home of the most powerful dragons. I'm what you may call a shifter. Not all in the land have this ability, but all the Draglen Brothers can.

There are other species, like vampires, who live on earth, but we are the only ones who can transport back and forth. We hold the power. If humans knew what really walked among them, they would treasure each other, rather than kill each other. I try to focus on my work, but keep seeing that girl Cess, pissed at me for walking her off the property. Her arms were so soft, and I could feel her anger. It's nice to have someone challenge you outside your family. I give orders in my land, and if they are not followed I take something, and it's always something vital like a wing or some claws. I have only had to put four down for death, but they pushed my buttons. Most of my people are kind and gentle, living among one another in harmony.

"Draken, we are going out to eat. Do you want something?" Showken asks. I can feel my other brothers at the door.

"Bring me something back, work needs to be done," I say, knowing my brothers and Showken are going looking for the females. Gemi and Layern will go with whatever Showken says, because he will make sure they all have a good time.

"I guess I'll order in," Showken says. I know this is a way to get me out with them, and I will not fall for it.

"When you order, make sure it's enough," I say, hearing the growls of the others, and Showken chuckling.

"Okay... I was wondering would you mind if I go down and check on Cess." Why would he want to do that? I go to the door to see his face. I open, and he and Layern are right there. Gemi is probably in his room.

"Why?" I glare.

"Why not?" Showken says, smiling hugely. I glare at Layern, as he already knows, and is waiting for my answer. That girl got under my skin, as soon as I saw her I wanted her.

"I think you should order some food and let me know when

it's here," I say, walking smoothly between my brothers and heading for the bar. I need a drink. The bar is already stocked and ready. The gift of being a dragon shifter is that once we have everything in the home, we can use our powers to place everything where it belongs.

"Hmm . . . I think you want her. Layern, what is the verdict?" Showken says.

"He wants her to scream his name," Layern says, shaking his head. He only has sex with humans to pass the time, not because he enjoys it. He says they are too fragile, and he gets tired of being gentle so that he won't kill them by accident.

"Draken, just for once, do what you feel, and not what's proper. If you want Cess to scream your name, make it happen. I mean, my name is screamed by many lips, and these human women enjoy being pleasured just as our women do," Showken says, shrugging his shoulders.

"Well, if I do want her I won't act on it, and besides, she would not be able to handle me," I say, wondering again, what if she could be in my bed. Those beautiful legs wrapped around me while her perfect lips open for me.

"Such a vivid, clear picture, Draken. I'm with Showken, you should just have that human and be done with it," Layern says.

"Stay out of my head and leave me alone about that girl, and if she sets one foot on this property I will send you back. Gemi and I can fix the issue and be back home. I'm done, Showken, and don't challenge my decision," I growl, and my brothers know that is the heir to the throne speaking and that conversation is over. Showken starts ordering food. Layern bows, showing respect, and leaves the room. I hate having to use that tone, but they keep pressing. That woman had better stay away from me. I'm not like some other guy. I walk over to the window and sniff. I can smell her from here. Her scent is so beautiful and enticing. Ravla is waiting for my return, to fulfill all of my desires. She knows not to expect any attachments. I'm already bound to marry someone, and nothing will change that. Ravla is just what I need; I may have to send for her, to get this Cess off my mind.

"Prince Draken, heir to the throne, dinner has arrived," Showken says. Showken is trying to make me feel bad; I will not.

"Thank you, Prince Showken; I shall be there in a minute. No one eats until I'm there," I say, to get a reaction. Showken will always disobey when I do things like that.

"Draken, when you come down I will be eating, so hurry your ass, or I might eat your meal as well," Showken says. I glare and he glares back. I can't help but smile. I will always need Showken. He reminds me to stay humble.

"Come on, I promise not to say anything about her," Showken smiles.

"Do you think Layern is angry, brother? I don't mean to offend, but that gift of his is too personal, and he should keep his mouth closed about certain thoughts," I say.

"I'm sure he is upset, nothing that you can't be forgiven for, just remember we are your brothers," Showken says, patting my back. I look at my brother, and wish I could be as laid back as he.

"I could never forget you all are my brothers. I just like privacy in my head," I say.

"You know he can't control it," Showken raises his brow.

"I know," I say, walking to the table and bowing to my brother, Layern, silently letting him know I'm sorry. We eat in silence. I look over and see that Gemi is uncomfortable. Gemi can be the nicest dragon you will meet, or he can be one of the meanest, it all depends on his mood. It comes in handy when we have to fight, when a challenge for the throne comes up. These six months cannot pass quickly enough. I will get Draglen Enterprises on the right track and get my brothers home. It's not always safe on earth; there is always the chance of being exposed. Usually humans stay away from us. The predator within us frightens them, even if they have no clue why. Showken uses his smile and mind control for the human females. My thoughts are interrupted.

"Draken, you know you meet your bride when we go home?" Gemi says. I can't keep up with this brother. Gemi is so confusing, switching from being shy to just talking out of the blue.

"Yes, I know," I say. I hear she has been groomed for me since birth. I wish she came with some experience; I have no patience for teaching.

"Brother, don't worry, she will be able to satisfy that hunger you have, I'm sure . . . unless-" Layern stops himself.

"Unless what?" I say.

"Unless you find that human too pleasurable to give up," Layern says, not looking up from his meal.

"Who said I-" I try to speak, but Showken is speaking.

"Draken, I know you, brother, you will have that female," Showken says. I glare at him.

"Ravla will come visit," I say, and I hear the chuckle.

"Are you still going to bang that female?" Showken murmurs. My favorite brother is pressing his luck. I glance over my shoulder, and can smell her scent again. She must have her window open. I will have Ravla come and occupy my time when I am not at the office. That will keep my mind away from this Cess girl. I hope.

CESS

I can't believe him. That Draken guy is the rudest guy I've ever met. He had no right to march me off the lawn like I'm a thief. He is gorgeous, but that attitude needs to go. Showken was way friendlier. This is why the promise is in place, men can be a distraction. I'm already spending too much thought on this Draken, whose light purple eyes are so extremely hot, and the body, with that long hair. Yikes, Draken smells like trouble and he most definitely looks like trouble. I will stay away from those brothers, even though Showken tried to say something, it's obvious who is in control. I need to get some studying done, anyway, my dream career and vacation are so near. I have just opened my statistics book and begun to do some homework when my phone rings. I look at the screen on my cell and see it's my best friend, Suzy.

"Hello."

"Cess, I think when we graduate I need a break from everything. Going to school, working and trying to party is too much work. I need to just relax for a year," Suzy says. Suzy is such a great friend. We have been friends since pre-school. Our parents are very close, and Suzy and I have been inseparable since we met. She always wants a break. I have basically coached her through college.

"Really? I think you would break from everything, except partying," I say, laughing.

"No, Cess, I'm serious this time. My parents are planning a huge vacation when I graduate in 3 months, to Europe. I was thinking I should do the same, except make mine a year," Suzy replies.

"Are you kidding, your father can afford to do that, he owns one of the biggest packaging factories in the world. You, on the other hand, have money because of your name only."

"Well, it doesn't matter why I have the money, as long as I have it." We both laugh, because Suzy is one of a kind. She is really smart, beautiful, and crazy.

"I get it, this all came on when you heard Luke and Cassie were getting married after college. I really hope not, Suzy, you can do so much better than Luke," I say. Luke and Suzy dated for the first two years in college, not to mention all through high school. I never liked Luke. He is a jerk and thinks he is God's gift to women. He always treated Suzy like crap, and I was happy when they broke up. She is so much better than him. I know she is still in love with him, and just hope she meets a great guy.

"You have no idea how that hurts, but I have been thinking about this for a while, and maybe . . . I might find a great guy on my vacation."

"Suzy, I hope you find a guy to get over Luke, even if it's an 'in the meantime' type of guy. I do think running away would not be good, and before you say you're not running, you are totally running."

"Whatever, what's new with you?"

"I was studying stats when you called, but we have new neighbors in Paradise Valley." I pause, remembering Draken and how much he pissed me off, yet I can't stop thinking about those beautiful eyes, light purple eyes. Why did he have to be such an ass?

"If you mention some neighbors, that means men! Do you finally have a date, because Cess, I think you need to move on from Travis."

"Yes, its men, fine, sexy-as-hell men, all brothers and by the way, no mentioning his name, remember?"

"Wait, how many brothers?"

"I saw four, but don't get your hopes up, the one in charge, Draken, is an ass. I will not be talking to them."

"Ohh, he already got under your skin, an ass huh? That may just mean you need to sleep with him, and everyone knows you have had no sex since Travis. This would be good for you."

"I don't do sex just because, you know that, and like I said, he is not just an ass. He is a gorgeous ass, which makes it worse, because I can see him being all cocky after he got the goods. Besides, I have made a promise, no men or sex. I'm staying focused on graduating with honors and starting my career."

"Ha! Cess, I think I need to get the girls together and we come over tonight to see these men. Are they all asses, or just the one you like?" Suzy says, laughing.

"Very funny, and no, the others were nice, and hot, but like I said, that Draken runs the show."

"We will see! I will get the girls and we will be at your house later, and maybe we can get them to come over. Your parents are still out of town, right?"

"Yes, but D is here, and you know how he gets."

"I can handle D. I want to meet the man that has caught your eye," Suzy says, with a sneaky laugh.

"I guess there is no getting out of this, I'll see you later. I need to get to working on these statistics."

"Okay, see you soon."

This is going to be a crazy evening. Why did I tell Suzy? She has no idea who she is dealing with. Draken walked me off the property. He has no sense of being a gentlemen in him. Besides, there is something weird about him and his brothers. They simply moved out of the way almost like a command was given. I might be crazy and just need to forget about Draken. My eyes need a break from working. I'm so glad I have this huge room with an area for dancing. Dancing always helps me relieve stress. I push out my chair and head towards my dance area. It has mirrors against the wall, with top of the line flooring. I dim the light and push the remote that controls the music. The song of choice comes on, and I start my dance. I close my eyes, feeling the beat, and let my body flow like waves, turning, spinning and twisting in a sensual way. My parents think I use this area for ballet, but my art is dancing from the soul, giving myself to the music and allowing my body just to move, without thought. I love dancing, and if I thought I could make a career out of it, then I would do it. My parents expect me to be a scientist and discover something great. I hear the money is good in being a scientist, yet my heart screams dance. I have an offer at one of the big research corporations in Arizona, working in a science lab. I would come in as a manager... amazing what my last name can get me, even if that is not what I want. The Lamil name is well known around the world. My great-grandfather was a very driven man, he acquired much land, starting wineries in Europe and expanding in the U.S. Durant Luke Lamil made sure that his hand was in everything. Today, the extent of the family wealth is unknown to the public, but I know we are worth well over a couple of billion. Money is not an issue with having a career, and in fact saving money is my idea. I don't want to get everything without working or saving, learning the value of money is important to me. That is why I choose not to go in the family business like my brother, but do something different, and although dancing is my true love, it would not be acceptable in any way, so science it is. This is really going to be a long day. I get back to work and finish the study I had planned for today.

"Hey, Suzy and the girls are coming over soon, can you please go put a shirt on?" I ask D, my nose tilted in disgust. My brother is a very handsome man, but the problem is he knows it, and right now his entire life is sleeping with everyone he can. I'm just glad he uses protection.

"Why sis, scared your friends might start drooling?" D laughs, as he eats his sandwich. The day has passed, and now it's four in the afternoon, and I'm sure D has been eating and playing games the entire time.

"Just put a damn shirt on."

"Ohh, somebody is still grumpy. Hey, Cess, you should feel alright, besides, getting involved after you-know-who would just make you miserable. Do I have to remind you of the scene you caused at the movies when you spotted that person?"

"How does any of that have to do with you putting on a shirt? And I was just being nice to the new neighbors."

"Right, and I didn't see you totally smiling at those guys with that "I'm available" smile," D says, in a girly voice.

"You get on my nerves, put the damn shirt on," I say, smiling. My twin is so annoying at times. He knows me so well, but I still have to give him a hard time.

"I will make sure I'm covered for your friends, who want me," D says laughing.

I decide to head to the pool house and get ready for a swim. I'm sure everyone will be up for swimming. I pass Gloria, the maid, and make my way to the pool house. I undress and take a shower before getting in the pool, I always do this, not a real reason behind this habit. The shower is perfect as I let the water cover my body, wetting my hair and face and just enjoying myself. I close my eyes, doing my meditation, until I feel a presence. I open my eyes and see no one, yet the feeling is strong. I shake off the weird feeling, and continue to relax under the water, until I smell the most intoxicating smell. It is amazing. I feel happy and curious. I look around again, and nothing. I turn back and it's like the presence is gone, but the smell remains, giving me a reminder. I wonder whether new flowers planted, or a new scent Gloria is using is what I smell, though that would not explain the feeling of being watched. No one is that stupid to come onto our property without permission, especially roaming the grounds. My father has ordered the guards to shoot first. The Lamils are not that nice about safety. I decide to forget the entire thing and get in the water. I put on my bathing suit and head to the pool, which is pretty impressive. Living in Paradise Valley does have its perks. As I get into the water and do a few laps, my mind drifts back to Draken. His long black hair and his beautiful eyes. I mean, the purple is so defined. I've never seen eyes like that, and his body is perfect. I know he has to be 6'6" at least, and all muscle. I wish I could have seen his smile, I bet it's gorgeous. I need to forget about Draken. Look at me, I can't even forget his name. I should not think about him, walking someone off your property makes it pretty clear where they stand with you. I just feel the need to know more. Why did his brothers let him do that, and why did they leave when he began to speak to me? I know it's not my business, but I've never been treated like that. He is probably just a miserable person. I will have fun with my friends; they should be here shortly. Gloria will send them this way. I will just relax until my friends come.

"Cess…" I hear Donna Marie calling my name. I turn, and see they are all in their bathing suits. Donna Marie, Suzy, Jamie, and Kelly look like models. I smile and shake my head.

"Yes, I see you all made it."

"Of course, when Suzy said you had men issues. I knew you needed an intervention. Now, where are these hot new neighbors?" Jamie says, smiling a wicked grin. She really has no shame at all.

"A man has your eye, Cess, yes, I want to meet this guy too," Donna Marie says. I love her so much. She is our party girl. She always has a reason to celebrate. If Donna Marie has her way, she will find a way to make a party out of this, and invite the new guys. I wonder if Draken would come. I'm pretty sure the others would if they knew.

"There's nobody who has caught my eye, besides, just one brother is a meany," I say, remembering the march off the property, which really pissed me off. He must not have a clue about who I am.

"Yeah, okay Cess, your face is giving away how this guy got under your skin. This is perfect - if you say he didn't make you melt, then let's have a party and invite him, along with other people, and see what happens," Jamie says. She truly believes that all men want her, and as long as protection is involved her motto is "young, sexy, and fun."

"Ohh, I can get a party together in no time. How about tomorrow night?" Donna Marie says, doing a shimmy with her hips.

"That will be fun; I just finished my final paper for Lit, so that would be perfect. *Lets party*!" Kelly says. Great, now there is going to be a party.

"Aww, come on, Cess, you know you want to, and besides, you may even get lucky with a guy," Suzy says, pouting.

"Fine, let's have a party, but don't say I didn't warn you about them. Now, who will invite them?" I say, making sure they know I will not be the one. I will not get marched off twice.

"I will, they don't have to worry about me, I…" Donna Marie says.

"We know, you're with Rich!" we all say in unison. I hope

this guy is the one, because she wants to run off and make little Rich's babies after college. I'm never being that devoted to a man, or anything else. Living the privileged life as we all are, we know first hand how you can't trust anybody. There is always a motive, and besides, Donna Marie is the one with all the family money. He could be using her, although for his sake I hope not; her brothers are crazy about their little sister.

"Let's go for a swim, I'll have Gloria bring some drinks out," I say. We all head for the pool. I can't believe I've been talked into a party where my new neighbors could be there, fantastic.

The girls and I are having a good time in the pool and talking about how each of us is glad this is our last year in college. Donna Marie says she will make sure to give them the address of the party for tomorrow night when she leaves. How did I get suckered? Draken probably won't show, and he'll make the others sit out. He is truly an asshole, a sexy asshole.

DRAKEN

Shit! That little girl just walked up and handed Showken a piece of paper saying we are all invited to a party tomorrow. I heard their entire conversation; the joy of having great hearing over long distances. The problem: so did my brothers, and if I know Showken, he is going, which will make Layern and Gemi go, then I will have to go, just to make sure trouble doesn't happen. NO! They are not going, six months and I will be home. I don't have time to watch them. Showken comes into my office, grinning.

"So, Draken, what you wearing to the party?" Showken says, laughing.

"Nothing," I respond.

"Really? I think that will impress the ladies."

"That Cess is really disturbing me. She just had to go run her mouth. We should not go to any party," I say, trying to convince my brothers. I know that Cess will be trouble. Her feelings are hurt because I walked her off the property. She's lucky that's all I did. I feel like something is going to happen, and this will not turn out good.

"Brother, why do you have such strong feelings about this girl? I mean, we always run into a curious one when we come to Earth, so why her?" Layern says, knowing the truth behind my frustration. I have never desired to be with a human woman, since my fatal encounter. Those legs, her smell and that smile could get her killed.

"I see, you know if you would just give in, maybe you could get rid of that frustration," Layern says.

"Ravla will be coming tonight, and any frustration I have will be dealt with then," I spit out.

"Ha," Showken says, tilting his head. "She will not satisfy you, brother, trust me on this; sometimes these human women have a pull you can't resist. Take her, have fun, and be done with it. Besides, you might have more fun than you think,"

"I want nothing to do with her at all," I say, "I may find her attractive, but I will never act upon it. She is nothing more than a child to me. I'm here on business, and Ravla can handle any other needs I may have." I end the conversation with a nod and make my way to the kitchen, finding I'm very angry. I can feel my back expanding; I must gain control fast, before this house is in shreds. I head to my room and beckon for Ravla to come now. I have the portal open for her in the bathroom. Ravla will make sure I forget that Cess. I smell her immediately.

"Ravla, nice to see your beauty," I say, as she walks through the door in a flowing red gown. Ravla is beautiful, with long, flowing, light orange hair, clear eyes, and a body that is perfect, not to mention she's the best Giver I've ever had.

"Hello, Draken," Ravla says, in that sensual voice. I know she will be able to make me focus. Shit, why am I thinking about anything but sexy Ravla's body?

"Is something wrong? I came as soon as I got your message," Ravla says, frightened.

"Oh, no, you're fine, it's me," I continue. "I know this is selfish of me, but I really don't want to talk; I just want to bury myself within you. Are you up for what I have planned?" I say, knowing she will do whatever I ask concerning sex.

"Of course, Draken, I love you within me. If this is the only way I can have you, then I will take it."

"Remove your gown." I see her excitement, and I can smell her arousal. Mmmm. "You have not been with another, right?"

"Oh Draken, how could you think I would. I love you," Ravla says, moving closer to me. She is totally naked, giving me a full view of her perfect round breasts, and those hips swaying my way. I will enjoy her today. I hate reminding her of my feelings, though.

"Ravla, I don't love, and you know that. However, I will show you much pleasure today and tonight. I need another drink, would you care for one?"

"No, I mean no thank you," she says.

Her feelings are hurt. Shit, I keep hurting people's feelings, especially Cess. I might have overreacted, but that girl gets me to boil, and I don't like that feeling. She is too damn sexy and I can't get those legs, those fabulous legs, out of my head. I so want them around me, as I take her over and over again. Fuck!

"Draken, are you okay?" Ravla asks, and I realize I'm thinking of how many ways I want to get into Cess. I knew that girl was going to be trouble.

"Yes, I'm fine."

"Well, you were saying something about a Cess, legs? What, or who, is that?" Ravla says, revealing irritation in her voice. This only inflames me, questioning me about anything is a no, especially if the person is not family.

"Make your way to my bed, Ravla, and question me no more. Is that clear?"

"Yes, Draken. I'm sorry for overstepping my bounds," she says, moving to my bed and spreading her legs, giving me access to view her arousal. I inhale deeply. Ravla has been my Giver for many years now. She knows what I like and how I like it. I should be over there having a good time, but instead I can't help but feel the need of Cess in my bed. Her skin is so soft; lick every inch of her is what I could do, taking my time to enjoy all of her, especially those legs. I find myself growling. I don't know when or how I make it to the bed, but I'm thrusting into Ravla, so fast that she doesn't have time to think. I hear her cry out in satisfaction, and I continue to take her, over and over again, thinking of Cess the entire time. Ravla will sense my disconnect, and I just hope she never finds Cess, or she will kill her.

***

The next morning, I look over and see Ravla sleeping. Her breathing is slow, which lets me know she's in a deep sleep. I get out of the bed, and notice my sheets are destroyed. Damn, even my bed has burn marks. Oh well, I guess I will be ordering a new one. I slip on my black silk pajama pants and head out of my room. I open the door and am greeted by Showken with a large glass of wine.

"Good morning," Showken says, grinning hugely. "I see Ravla is here, umm, I think we need to talk, brother." The chuckling continues as he turns and walks away from my room. I walk behind him, not speaking, drinking down the wine. Drinking wine keeps my temper under control. In my land I have other ways to do that, but here, wine is what helps, or any alcoholic drink, really. My beast needs to be under control. Making my way to the study, I see Layern and Gemi, which means something is up.

"What's wrong?" I say.

"You, that's what's wrong," Gemi says. I look at my brothers, then close my eyes to think, remembering they can see my sexual acts if I choose, only through the mind, though. Cess was on my mind the entire time with Ravla. This is not good. Fuck!

"I told you, have her. The way she was looking at you before you walked her off the property, there will not be any convincing involved," Showken says.

"Layern, you're quiet, do you agree? Before you answer, I don't want you telling me anything about what I think, clear? I just want your opinion on my taking a human woman for pleasure. And, remember, I have only done this once, so the likelihood of my killing her is very strong," I say sternly. I'm tired of all this talk about a human.

Layern studies my face, and when he speaks, his tone is guarded. "Well, based on your experience with our women, your patience with the people in the land, and the fact you vowed not to kill any more humans, I think that you should get her out of your system. While we are here getting the business in order, Cess could be your Giver, instead of Ravla. Besides, you thought about Cess while destroying Ravla, she's TKO!" Layern says, smiling.

"Interesting, you all want me to have this girl. What if she falls in love?" I ask.

"After you have your fill of her, just go back to being the ass you are, and she will stop loving you instantly, brother," Showken says, with that stupid grin on his face.

"Listen, you have Ravla here and that doesn't keep your mind off her, so just have that girl, as you call her," Gemi says, irritated.

"I will give your thoughts some consideration, but right now my Giver is here, and I plan on taking. I know you all plan on going to the party. I can still hear all my brothers if I choose, so if I detect any problems, Gemi, I will punish every one of you for all mistakes. We cannot risk anyone's curiosity. Thank you, brothers, now I'll be getting some food and heading back, Monday is all business," I say, glaring at each brother. I don't give anyone a chance to respond, but Showken yells as I walk away "I bet she will feel real good, brother!" I truly hate Showken sometimes. I know that if I didn't have this pull towards Cess, she would already be in Showken's bed. I make my way back to Ravla.

I look at my ravished bed and smile with pride. She will wake soon, and I will finish my time with her. Ravla takes what I give with no complaint. I will always keep her, even after my marriage. I turn on the shower, just climbing in, as my body heat is enough to warm me. Why is Cess on my mind? Why do I desire her so? That should not be. I will keep Ravla around to keep me focused. It will only be six months, and then I will be home, away from her. The next trip I will pick the area, Gemi's choice is costing me my sanity.

CESS

I can't believe they actually invited them. Now, I'm going to a party where Mr. Walk You Off His Property may be there. Well, I won't be humiliated this time, and seeing him again might cure this feeling I have about him. It may only be because it's been months since I've had sex. Like, he is the most handsome man I have ever seen. Who wouldn't want that man? I need to have on the perfect outfit. If I know Donna Marie, Travis will be there. I so wish Travis would fall off the face of the earth. Travis and I were dating for the first 2 ½ years of college, until I caught him kissing Lauren. I thought we would get married one day, and he broke my heart. I trusted his "I love you," and it was nothing but a lie. The more I think about that hurt, the more I know getting involved with anyone is out of the question, especially Draken. Wanting him should be far from my mind, yet there is something different about him, in fact about them all. I've never seen one man controlling his family, the way they all dispersed. I know in the Lamil family, my dad can be very demanding, but with Draken, they never said a word, and it's almost like they knew to leave; my dad doesn't possess that type of power. It is another hot day here in Paradise Valley, Arizona, the temperature is reaching over 115 degrees today. I know that the party will lead to the pool at some point, so I will make sure to pack a sexy swimsuit. Hmm, I think my pink and black bikini, the one with hints of glitter in the material, will be perfect. Yes, I'm going to be hot! I will make that Draken drool, and then I won't even speak to him. That will teach him never to treat me that way again. I feel like dancing. I walk over to my iPod, place my earplugs in and start moving. I love to dance. Dancing is a release of many things, and right now, dancing will help make sure my nerves are under control for the party. The way I dance is a mixture of ballroom with ballet and hip-hop. If my parents saw me grinding right now, they would think I'd lost it. I just love the freedom of dancing. When I feel the tap on my shoulder I jump, because everyone knows if you knock and I don't answer, that just means no company is wanted. I turn and it's my twin. D never gives me any personal space.

"What is the rule?" I say, as I turn down the music.

"You know rules don't apply to me, sis, I just want to know if we are riding together to the party tonight."

"You're not going."

"Yes, I am. You know that parties don't happen unless I'm there. Besides, I want to see this guy that's got you dancing again. I want you back dating again, since Travis you have been different."

"What did I say about his name? You need to ride by yourself to the party, I might stay over at Donna Marie's house. Now get out," I say, feeling horrible for speaking to D like this.

"Hey listen, Cess, you're my twin sister and best friend. I'm sorry, but I want you happy again. I don't want you to not open up because of him. Now don't be mad, and come give your brother a hug," he says, smiling, arms wide open waiting for my hug.

"I'm not hugging you, D, you're not fooling me. As soon as I'm in your arms you're going to lick my face. Ugg, and that's gross by the way."

"The ladies love it."

"That's only because they're delusional," I say, smiling.

"Well, I'm glad we got this all clear, now I need to go get ready for the party, sis. And, umm, just in case you were wondering what to wear, I think that silver dress thingy will make heads turn," D says, walking out of my room. I yell out, "Thanks D, love."

"Any time!"

I head to my big closet, and sit on the bench looking at all my silver dresses. I choose the short, backless one. I decide to be different, and add blue heels and accessories. This is going to be a night to remember. I plan on having a good time.

***

Dressed and ready to party, I grab the keys to one of the many cars in the garage. I see I have the Maserati Convertible keys. Yes, this will be perfect! When Draken sees what he missed out on, he's going to kick himself. I grab my packed bag, and make my way to the car. Gloria always makes sure the car is brought around. She tells Gordon, who is the driver, to ensure the car is ready to drive.

I jump in, and waste no time speeding past Draken's house. I still feel embarrassed about how I was treated, but this party will redeem me, and it will be Draken wishing he could have me. Ha! I don't have to drive very long before I'm in front of Donna Marie's house. I pull up and my car is taken away for parking. I head in and go straight to the music, I start dancing, moving very slow. Dancing alone can be so fun at times, and you get to see the reaction of the guys, and ladies. I hear Suzy before I see her.

"Cess, Cess!" Suzy yells over the music. As I turn, she is dancing towards me. Suzy and I are the best dancers among our friends. They all think they're too proper to do what we do. There is never shame in our dancing, just freedom. She finally reaches me, and we are dancing and talking.

"You look fabulous! Every guy here is going to want you," Suzy says.

"You are the one who looks amazing, that blue fitted dress is painted on, and I can see every curve. You wouldn't be trying to catch someone tonight?"

"Maybe, I've got to go mingle. Have fun! I'm sure your neighbor boys are coming. Donna Marie is very convincing," Suzy says, grinning. What the hell did she say? Before I can ask her, she's gone, moving through the people. I move away from the dance floor, just walking around. I really enjoy Donna Marie's house. It's very lavish, like ours. I take a walk around, and finally spot him. Bitch! He is all over her, and they look as if they are in love. That's how we were until she got her little slutty hands on him. I should watch them make out. I need to go. So much time has passed, yet I can't get over Travis. I hate that name. I truly loved him, and my heart still breaks, watching him kiss and love another. I spent all that time hoping I could be his everything, when all along he was passing time with me, and really wanted Lauren. Lauren is pretty, but I would never have guessed it. He still looks so good. He notices me staring as he kisses her neck. The eye contact is instant, so I flip him off. He just gives Lauren a deep kiss, tugging at her hips. Damn, I miss sex. Turning, I go to an empty area, and let the tears fall as I sit on a bench. I don't realize I'm sobbing until I hear a voice, I'm crying so hard. I just ignore the person, hoping he leaves. Then hands are on my shoulders, caressing me. I don't look to see who it is, I'm happy that someone is not telling me to get over it. Then, his mouth is next to my ear.

"Hello, Cess, who made you cry?"

"Showken?" I say, leaning away, oh my, does he look tasty. Why is he here? Oh yeah, Donna Marie.

"Who made you cry?" Showken asks again. I'm so astonished at his deep green eyes, I don't notice the other brothers walk up. Oh, I'm surrounded by hot men, that will surely make me feel better!

"Hi, Showken. It's nothing, just seeing someone who hurt me, it can be a little too much at times." I say, wiping my face with a handkerchief out of my handbag.

"So, this man was your ex?" Layern says. Wow, how did I remember his name? He looks at me so caringly. I wonder if Draken is here too.

"No, he's not here."

"Shit!" I say, jumping back. How the hell did he know that? "How did you know what I was thinking?" I ask.

"I didn't, your body can tell me a lot, besides, I have what you might call strong perception." Layern says, smiling.

"Where is this guy that makes such a beautiful lady cry?" Showken asks, searching my eyes. I look around and see the other brothers' eyes roaming over my body. Wow, at least someone wants me.

"Don't worry about him, Showken, I'm fine. I think I'm going home," I say, turning to leave, but he pulls me back in front of him. I know these men are going to be trouble.

"Wait, we just got here, and we want to dance," Showken says, smiling, and I see those dimples again. Yikes!

"We? I mean, I'm sure all the ladies would like to dance with you guys," I say, blushing. They are just a bunch of sexy hot men. I really need to leave.

"Showken, just tell her," Gemi says, looking at me.

"Tell me what?" Oh shit! What are they not telling me?

"We are here to have fun, but also to see if you like our brother, Draken," Gemi says, cocking his handsome face to the side. I notice they all are waiting for an answer. Why didn't the asshole bother to come? Why send his brothers? I frown.

"He doesn't know. We are trying to help him out of his shell, so to speak," Layern says, smiling. All this attention is going to have this girl going crazy. I look from brother to brother, and there's something different about them. I know they are fine, and brothers, but they look like they could be very dangerous.

"Umm, I... well, since it doesn't seem like you're going to let me leave, I guess let's go dance!" I say, moving from the corner they have me in. I glance over my shoulder and smile. "I hope you can dance, because that's my specialty." I walk away towards the music and party people. I feel them right behind me, and I know they are there, there is a sense of danger there too. I hope they are not serial killers. I turn and look, and all smiles is what I see, as they walk like kings. I walk to the floor and begin to move. One of my favorite songs is playing, Ride, by Ciara. I feel hands on me as I'm dancing, and Showken is behind me. Wow, he can really dance, moving to my pace and never missing a step. This guy is really good! I close my eyes, feeling the song, as I feel another set of hands coming from in front, and there is Gemi dancing with me, and he is grinding on me like we are alone. Yikes, I'm so in trouble. I turn my head, and see Layern mouth "my turn next." These guys are walking sex. That's as simple as I can put it. If you look up sex, it will have all their pictures, especially Draken. I wonder why he is not here? He must not like me. Showken is whispering softly in my ear.

"My brother Draken wanted us to check you out. Make sure before he asks you out that you are a big girl."

"What does that mean, a big girl?" He looks at me, and arches a brow as he chuckles. I see my friends laughing and eyeing them. Gemi makes me focus on him when he starts going down to the floor, making sure to rub his big, hot hands down my legs. This is a fantasy! Showken persists.

"Well, Cess, it's up to you. My brother wants you, he will take you on dates, buy you gifts, and treat you well. You have to be willing to share this body with him," he whispers, as he turns me quickly, and now I'm facing him. Gemi is having a good time with me from behind. What are they doing, and what is he asking me to do, exactly?

"What are you saying, Showken?" I say, looking him in his eyes. I'm trying to have an attitude, but he is so damn sexy.

"I mean," he says, "You are sexual when you're dancing, and before you answer: the way you are dancing lets me know you are not a virgin," Layern walks up, pushing him and Gemi away. They find new dance partners, the ladies and guys are staring at all three of them. Layern totally takes control of the dance as a new song comes on. He picks me up, and pulls my legs around his waist, and lays his hand on my belly, pressing me to lean back. I lean back, feeling the music, and now the dance is pure heat. It's dirty dancing, with an R rating. I'm having a good time when he, too, asks me about Draken.

"I'm sure my brother has told you about Draken."

"No, he has only asked if I will screw your brother!" I snap.

"I see you're upset," Layern says, moving me slowly. "but you can't deny you want him, right? Cess, I know you think Draken is an ass, yet you still want him. You're young, nobody is saying you have to marry him. Our brother likes you. He just doesn't know how to tell you, and that's where we come in. You are new to him, Cess; you have a brother, wouldn't you do anything for him?" I return the movements, letting him know I can dance too. I'm not up for sale, and I don't care how handsome they are or how well these guys can dance, smile, and especially tempt me to make me go back on my promise. Their asshole brother can go to hell. I'm not dating or accepting gifts, and mostly definitely not screwing him.

"No, no I'm not dating your brother." I say, pulling away. "You and your brothers can find another slut. I choose to be single, and not because offers don't come in on a regular basis. I'm Cess Lamil, and you need to look that up. I don't need any gift, or anything he can do for me. I can provide for myself." I walk away, going to speak with my girls. The more I think about it, the more pissed off I get. I walk up to Suzy, Jamie, and Kelly, who are gawking at my new sexy neighbors. I don't think they even see me. Jamie is more the type they need, for what they're asking.

"Hello!" I say, waving my hands in their faces. They are all staring.

"Cess, please tell me you're going to go to bed with one of them tonight?" Kelly says, waving. I stand in front of them, placing my hand on my hip.

"You can have them! They are here trying to fix me up with their brother, Draken, but want to make sure that I give up the cookies. What kind of-" I say.

Before I can finish, Jamie is fussing. "Cess, you are so stuck on yourself. They should be protecting The Great Draken. I'm surprised you haven't heard of him. If they are here on his behalf, consider it a privilege. You should watch the business world more closely. Draken and his brothers run Out of World Enterprises; it's the third largest company in the world. I know you come from

42

money, but the joke is, they are the money. You see where I'm going with this?" Jamie says, still smiling at them. I turn, and see all their eyes are on me. Why?

"Jamie, maybe you should do it, I don't want to, and you know all about him, go for it," I say.

"Jamie, if you won't, I will," Kelly says, freshening her lip gloss. "Oh shit, here comes one."

I turn, and Showken is there smiling at everyone. I have to stay away from him, and his brothers. I see Travis looking at me and his face says it all, jealousy. Yes! That is what I want him to feel.

"Hello, beauties! Can I steal Cess for one second, and then may I have a dance with you, Kelly? My brother would like to dance with you now, Jamie." Showken says, placing his hand in mine and walking me to one of the many balconies in Donna Marie's house. Where is Donna Marie? If I have to guess, she and Rich are somewhere having sex. They are like rabbits.

"I said no!"

"I say, yes," Showken says.

"Why are you bothering me about this?" I frown.

"Look, we are only here for 6 months, then we're gone. Listen, it's not an insult, actually we think very highly of you. We just want our brother happy, but if your answer is still no, we will not say another word. I do ask, though, if you would not mind coming to a party at our house next weekend. Draken spends most of his time at the office, so will you come?" He does that smile, and the dimples are my weakness. "Yes, I will come."

"Thanks, Beautiful, now I'm off to have fun with Kelly," Showken says, leaning in, and giving me a kiss, and then he whispers "Your ex is boiling mad, but that will teach him about breaking ladies' hearts." He walks away. I take a deep breath, trying to process all of this. I have just been asked to date Draken, and to make sure my body is at his disposal. WOW! I hear some crazy things, but this is number one. He is the finest man I've ever seen. How did Showken know my girlfriends' names? Maybe they were introduced earlier, and Jamie seems to know all about them. Draken is all man. No, I will not set myself up for heartache, besides, why would I enter a six-month sexual relationship. I want long term, marriage, and maybe a couple of kids. I don't want to just have a roll in the hay. Call me old-fashioned, I want it all. I decide to eat something, and head for the buffet.

I feel a bump. "Hey, sis, I see you getting your groove on the dance floor. Everyone is talking about Cess, and the three guys you were dancing with, even Travis," D says, grabbing a handful of cocktail shrimp.

"D, I really don't want to talk about it," I say, sighing heavily. "I'm going to head home. I just want to sleep," I close my eyes and see him standing in the door with that jet-black hair, and those light purple eyes, he has a presence that speaks volumes. His brothers do too, but Draken is in control. I mean, he made sure I was off the property, and when Showken tried to speak up, he was quieted. I still don't get that, why would they obey him if they run the business together?

"Hey sis, you just got here." D says, smiling and hugging me. "Don't let the neighbors, Travis or anyone else run you off. You're a Lamil and the first-born girl. Besides, your twin is here, anybody giving you a problem I can handle them. I didn't stop my martial arts training like you."

I stay for a little while longer, deciding to sneak away later. I drive home, take a hot shower, and climb into bed thinking of Draken. Maybe I need to experience this to put in my Bio for later in life. I do know Draken has a pull on me, and I would love to be under his body, or even on top. "Draken, you really make a girl warm." I turn over, and fall asleep quickly.

DRAKEN

Fuuuuck! Why did they go to that party? They know what they are doing. Going to the party, and sending me vivid images of Cess in that dress, showing off those legs. Damn! Ravla is still here, and that should be my focus, yet that damn girl is still in my head. I have never wanted a human so badly in my life. Humans always make me disgusted with their superior attitude. Ha! If they only knew! Taking Cess as a Giver could cost her her life. I vowed, the last time I killed a human trying to be with one, that I would never do that again, it's too painful to talk about. Being with Cess for long periods of time, I'm just not sure. Besides, being with me would mean so much more than she could ever understand. My brothers were very kind about showing me her facial expressions, when it came to me. She doesn't know her face was red when Showken and Gemi danced with her. She is very nice to look at. The way her hips were grinding it was like a slow stir, very tender, and sexy. I could grind her too. These conflicting feelings are not what I expect out of my entire 427 years. Yet, this female human has me wanting her. That beautiful brown hair needs to be fisted in my hand. Travis needs to be taught a lesson. Showken and Layern will be dealt with later for their proposition of Cess being with me. She finds me disgusting, and shows no interest in me at all. I see she left the party early. I wonder why.

"Ravla, you are truly amazing; I so enjoy when you please me. Thank you for coming, but I must get started on my work. If I need you again, I will send a message. The portal is ready," I say, opening the bathroom door with my mind. The portal is open; she just needs to walk through, so I can go see Cess while she sleeps, and maybe visit her in her dreams.

"Yes, of course, Draken. I look forward to your next request. I will always be your Giver if you want me," Ravla says, bowing. As she reaches the portal, she turns and smiles. I hope she can be my Giver always, but Cess is who I want as a Giver right now. The problem is that I can't tell her what all that means, or she will think I'm some crazy guy. I love our tradition, and it's very much an honor to be chosen as a Giver.

"Take care, Ravla. Remember, no other touch than mine, or you know what happens."

"Yes, Draken." She walks through the portal, and it closes immediately behind her. Ravla is no fool, I'm sure she can sense my need for another. She knows the rules though, I can have more than one Giver. After having a shower I lie across my bed, wiping away Ravla. Closing my eyes, I enter Cess' room very slowly. Another benefit of being a Dragon shifter is being able to enter any place without being seen. I want to see her and smell her scent again. I'm not sure if she is Giver material, but if I want her, then she will be mine. If only she were not human; that is the problem when and if I take her to Cortamagen, and it's a very dangerous problem. Her room says "girl" all around. I see she has books, music, and dance pictures everywhere. She's not a neatness fanatic. Hmmm, I see she is dedicated to her studies. When I glance at her bed, she looks peaceful, and sexy as hell. She stirs in her sleep, and I know I have to see what she is dreaming about, this may help me to decide if she's worth pursuing. A person's dreams can say a lot about her, showing how she will behave day to day. Humans have this need to dismiss dreams, but in my world, a dream is the truth of what one may want to happen. I enter her dream, and see her dancing on stage, interesting. I watch as her dream progresses into a place on the beach, where she is crying. I wonder why? I should make my presence known. I walk up the beach, and notice her mingled shock and pleasure. I need to know why she's crying; it's a dream to her, and she will never know I was really here.

"Why are you crying, Cess?" I ask. She turns, and her face is all flushed. Wow, she is beautiful.

"I'm not sure," she says, blinking at me. I sit next to her, and place my arms around her, comforting her. I feel myself getting solid like a rock. Damn! It's a dream, no harm in playing. Her body is too perfect. I start with her neck, kissing and sucking very gently. She turns, placing her lips on mine, and I start to suck her upper lip, moving quickly for her tongue.

She tastes extremely good. I could feast on her all day and night. When I hear the word "Yes" moaned, I know I am good to go. I remove her top and bottom, laying her down. Her breasts are perfect for my hand. Her nipples are a dark brown; I must taste them. I squeeze, and she gives me the answer I want. Her cry for more is all I need. I place my mouth around her left breast, sucking and pulling, making sure she can feel my heat. Cess' response to me is really good, a Giver she will be.

"Please?" she asks. I chuckle, because I feel her humping my leg. I will have this girl, but not in a dream.

"Please what?" I ask. I want her to say it. She needs to admit her want, and her desire for me. I want her as a Giver. I need to know everything she wants.

"Please, can you make me come," she demands, with her mouth open, and eyes closed. Who is this girl? Those words coming from her mouth are sexy. She will be my downfall, but I will give her a release. "Draken, I want you."

"I know, now you're going to get real hot baby, but don't worry, you will come," I say, placing my hands on her lower belly. I release a heat through my hand, she screams out in satisfaction. I know I will need to hear that more often. "Yes, scream for me," I say, moving my head down to taste her sex. She is delicious. If I had known human women tasted so good, I would have taken a human Giver. I let my tongue clean her thighs, and her sweet arousal, making sure every drop is gone. She continues to squirm, making me want her more. Maybe she will be what I need. Now I've had a taste, and seen she wants me too, I will make her a Giver. I stand up, placing a kiss on her soft lips, and leave the dream. Before I leave her room, I decide to leave her a gift. I place my hand on a piece of paper on her desk, leaving my mark.

"Cess, I'll come for you soon," I say, leaving her room. Opening my eyes, I smell my hands, inhaling deeply. Oh yes, I want to taste more. Placing my fingers in my mouth, I suck all that I can get of Cess. I will take a shower, and then I will decide when I should take her. Cess out of the dream will not like my rules, Cess in the dream is amazing.

I will figure this out. I will start on work, though. My needs will have to wait, business is always first. Heading for the shower I hear my brothers, and smell their company. They had better make sure nothing weird happens, or they will have me to deal with. Showering, I feel my brother's presence.

"What?" I ask.

"Did you see Cess? I sent as much as possible. She wants you, and I think having her as a Giver will help you understand the humans better," Showken says, smiling.

"Whom did you bring home?" I glare.

"Oh, that's one of Cess' friends, Kelly. I will have fun with her tonight," Showken says, rubbing his hands together.

"Just make sure you don't kill her or let her fall for you, and please disguise your face, so she thinks she's with someone else. Make sure to spread the message," I say, still washing.

"I'm sure they can hear, and Layern didn't bring anyone," Showken says, cocking his head, letting me know he is still having a problem. "Hey, umm brother, when I came in the house I smelled Ravla and Cess. Why is that?"

"Get the fuck out, Showken."

"Okay, tell me the details later, but you're going to make Cess your Giver, aren't you?"

"GET OUT!"

"Okay, I have a date waiting," Showken says, backing out, his hands held up in surrender.

"Remember, work starts tomorrow, so get what you can tonight. Have them gone before I rise in the morning," I say, knowing he can hear me as well as the others.

Climbing out of the shower, I grab a towel, drying my hair, and going to air-dry on my bed. I quickly remember I have not spoken with Timothy, our manager. I need to call him. I reach for my phone to make the call. He knows to answer when I call, day or night.

"Hello, Mr. Draglen, what can I do for you?" Timothy says, nervously. He has been with the company for 10 years, never questioning our age or any of the things he has seen.

"I will be at the office tomorrow morning, please have everyone's files on my desk."

"Yes sir, I will make sure they're there waiting for you," Timothy says. I can hear his breathing becoming faster.

"I'm not pleased with the numbers from the last six months. I think some people will be leaving, Timothy. I hope you're not one, since I think you work really hard, but we are losing money in our investments, and that means we should invest in other places. Someone dropped the ball, and someone will pay."

"I understand, Mr. Draglen."

"I'll see you tomorrow." I hang up before he can say goodbye. I don't plan on firing Timothy, but frightening him is always a joy. I don't ever want him comfortable. When humans get comfortable, they become lazy, and if that happened, he could say things about me and my brothers that could be damaging.

I would have to kill Timothy, so frightening him works; I will always do it. Sleep is what I need now, and what I will have. I close my eyes, remembering Cess and the sweetness of the lovely gift she gave me, letting out all that sweet juice for me, what a great drink to have. I will handle business, and then I will see if she is willing to be a Giver.

***

When we walk into our office the next morning, my brothers and I are acknowledged with smiles all around. I have no time for this. Of course, I notice all these human women smiling and blushing, and I can even smell them getting wet. My brothers and I do have an effect on women.

The question is, would they feel the same if they saw our other aspect? We walk to my office. Timothy is waiting for me with stacks of files. I look out of the window. Turning, I see the three stacks on the desk. "Which stack relates to finances?" I ask, darkly.

"Umm, it's the last stack, umm Mr. Draglen."

"How many are there?" I ask, knowing the answer already. There are 85 people in total who work in finance department.

"It's 85 people, sir," Timothy says, taking out a handkerchief to wipe his forehead. Timothy is an average guy, who, if he didn't suspect we were more than human, would not be this loyal. I'm sure he stays because of the pay, and the threat of not knowing who I truly am.

"Fire the first 50 files in this pile," I say, looking at him. With no hesitation he moves, counts 50 and places them on a chair.

"I will not deal with incompetence, Timothy; you go handle those files now, and have them off the property in one hour," I say. I don't have to say I'm done, he knows me well enough just to go do it. I like Timothy as a manager. I would never get rid of him, and if he were in my land I would give him the title of Leka, this would make him pretty high in my land. His loyalty would be rewarded, but this is not my land, and the only thing I can ensure is his job and safety. He's watched, so nothing happens to him. I don't want him being in car accidents, or anything that could interrupt his work.

"Yes sir, I will make sure it's done within the hour," he says, leaving.

"Oh, make sure to alert Cindy that I'm back and need her in my office."

"Yes, sir." He is gone. I turn my attention to the numbers of Out of World Enterprises. Our company is slipping in gross by 2.3%, and that's unacceptable. My father says anything over 2 % and you can be in danger. There are always companies coming up. We must stay ahead to ensure our place. I smell her coming before she knocks.

"Come in," I say. Cindy walks in, carrying a glass of wine from our cellar and smiling hugely. She has a crush on me, and never tries to hide it. She is always wet when she's around me. It's very distracting to smell arousal all day long, so I usually send her to Showken or Gemi.

"Hello Mr. Draglen, it's so good to have you back in town. The company is never the same when you're not here. I'm at your disposal!" Cindy says, smiling. I really thought she would lose interest, yet every time I have come to town for the last four years, she has still wanted me to take her to bed. It's never going to happen. Cindy is an attractive woman. She is medium height with short blonde hair, and has an okay body. I just don't like women chasing me.

I'm naturally a predator and I like prey, not another predator, and she is hunting me. Other reasons are, I don't do humans, and for two, she has an addictive personality. No one should be addicted to me. I'm not your average guy. I take a sip of the wine, looking at her.

"Cindy, listen, first please stop giving me the, "I want to screw you" eye, and second, I need a report on how to get numbers up in the next three months. Do you think you can handle all of what I just said?" I say, hoping she gets it. I don't want to fire Cindy, but I will have her walked out of my building if she continues her flirting.

"Yes, I totally understand, Mr. Draglen. I will get right on that report. I look forward to having you around also, sir; it's always a pleasure to be in such good company."

"Cindy, one day you will be escorted out for harassing the boss." I say, glaring. It does nothing but make her more intrigued with me. I really need to have her evaluated for mental problems. I think sometimes she could be aware of the danger with me and like it.

"I will get you the report ASAP, sir." Cindy says, leaving, as she now understands my tolerance for her today is extremely low. This is going to be a long 6 months. Maybe Cess will help, being a Giver.

CESS

Whoa! What the hell kind of dream was that? All of that talking with Showken about being with Draken has got to me. I can't believe my dream. I need a shower. What the hell is that sticky feeling between my legs? As I'm opening my legs to feel, I smell him all over me. Ohh, how much did I drink last night? I'm pretty sure I didn't bring Draken to my house, yet his scent is everywhere on me. I really need a shower now. Walking to my shower, I notice a piece of paper on my desk. It looks like a picture; staring in amazement, I see a picture of beautiful purple wings. They are so detailed and look so real. I sniff the paper for some reason I can't explain, and smell him on the paper. Holy shit!! This dream is getting creepier. I head to the shower, and get in as soon as the water heats up. I stand there forever, trying to figure out why I smell like Draken, and better yet, why I can remember that smell so well. I try to think of an explanation, only to come up empty. Showken is trying to set me up with him. Draken made it pretty clear that he didn't want me to come onto his property. I should never have agreed to come over this weekend. This is why I said no men for a while. I'm not even with Draken, and my thoughts are all about him. I'm going to cancel for this weekend. I'm just going to continue to study. Draken may be sexy and handsome, and have a great body, but he also is a very mean man that I want nothing to do with. I will control my hormones, although they are craving a man's touch. Draken, no way will I seek him out. I finish my shower, getting dressed, and stride to the kitchen. I hear my parents, they're home from a business trip.

"Hello, Mom, Dad. How was the trip?" I say, grabbing a seat at the counter. Vikki, our cook, is making breakfast. I like to cook, but when my parents are home, Vikki is the cook if they're eating.

"Hello, Princess!" my Dad says, coming to give me a kiss on the cheek. My father's name is Don Lee Lamil, after his great grandfather. I really hate when they use my real name. I mean, really, who names their daughter Princess? I'm the only girl among the grandchildren on my father's side of the family. That still doesn't matter; I never go by the name Princess, except around my parents.

"Where is your brother?" my mother asks. She is truly an

awesome mom to have. She is so lovely to be around. I hope one day to be as graceful as she is. My mother's name is Jaclyn. I love her name; it's very fitting for her. My mom is a beauty right out of a movie.

"I don't know; he might still be asleep. We both went to Donna Marie's house last night. She had a few friends over," I say, as my breakfast is placed in front of me. Yum, French toast and fruit!

"Did you and Duke have a good time?" my dad asks, just as D comes rolling in from a night of partying. Yes, my parents named us both names we hate. I always tell D, though, his name is better than mine, there are many men named Duke, but look at me, my name is Princess. That is what you call your daughter, not name her. I'm thankful that they didn't name me what my grandfather wanted, because D and I are twins. He thought my name should be Duchess, to match Duke.

"Hey mom, hey dad. Vicki, can you just get me some juice, no food for me this morning," D says, squinting. Clearly, my brother was out having a good time. I had a good time too, even better in my dream. No, I'm not going to think about that.

"Duke, I'm glad to see you. No need to ask how much fun you had last night," my dad says, smiling.

"I'm going to take my juice back to my room. I need sleep. Glad to see you, Mom and Dad. Oh, Cess, you were the talk of the party, dancing with those guys," D says, chuckling as he walks away. He did that on purpose. My father doesn't want me dancing, speaking, or talking with a man he doesn't know. I hate being the girl sometimes.

"What guys were you dancing with?" my dad says, looking right at me with those grey eyes. Damn it! I just eat, and try to ignore the question. My father's affairs in the business world are widespread, and his way of getting information is by any means he can.

"Oh, Don, leave her alone, you know Princess is very smart. You can't allow Duke to do whatever, and try to restrain her," my mom says, patting my arm as if she can stop my father's interrogations. Never.

"Princess, what guys?" he asks again.

"I'm glad you are dating again," Mom says gleefully. "That Travis boy broke your heart, and I always thought you were too good for him anyway. I think you should date Marlon. He comes from a fabulous family, and he's very handsome, your kids will be adorable." She is so into making sure I get married to a "well-to do" guy, and making sure he looks good, so her grandchildren will look fabulous. I love her, but sometimes she can be shallow. Wait, she only wants the best for me. I shouldn't be mean, she's not doing twenty questions with me.

My mom, when I turned 16 yrs old, took me to the doctor and placed me on the pill, saying "Don't tell your dad, but I don't want you making any mistakes by getting pregnant." I have been off the pill since I broke up with Travis. I'm not having sex for a while, although Draken. Why is he always in my thoughts?

"I said, what guys?" He frowns.

"We have new neighbors in the Haltons' old house. Donna Marie invited them to her party to be nice. I just danced with them, Daddy, to be nice. I'm focused on my schooling. You have nothing to worry about," I say, trying to stop the questions. It must work, because my father's face softens as he comes around the counter, placing a hand on my shoulder.

"I just don't want people taking advantage of you. Princess, you were born into a wealthy family, and many times guys will get close to you to get to me. I have to protect you. You understand, right?"

"Yes, Dad, of course," I say, finishing my breakfast as fast as possible. I need to ease my father's mind. "You don't need to worry about these guys. I was told they are the owners of Out of World Enterprises."

"What! Those guys are in town? The Draglen brothers are very successful men, honey. See, I told you our daughter is smart. Good pick," Mom says, nodding at me.

"I'm not dating any one of them. I just want to finish school and start my career," I say, pushing away from the counter. It's time to go, and I really owe D for this talk. Thanks, twin brother. This is going to be a long week, with my brother on at me about these guys. My father must have thought they were okay, because after our conversation he goes right to his laptop and starts working. I don't care who this guy is, I want nothing to do with Draken, I think. My dreams say different.

***

Friday comes quickly. I'm so happy it's the weekend and I'm caught up on school work. I'm staying in and enjoying the pool. I just want to relax. I go to the family room and turn the television on. I never watch T.V., but there's a show on about dancing that caught my interest. I watch it, and end up falling asleep until I hear Gloria.

"Ms. Cess, you have a visitor at the door. He says his name is Show, umm Show . . . "

"Showken?" I ask.

"Yes, that's it. Shall I escort him in?" Gloria asks.

"Yes, that's fine," I say, rubbing my hands over my hair. Why is he here? I'm not going over to his place. I glance at the clock and its 8:30 p.m., no way.

"Ms. Cess, Showken," Gloria announces. I turn, and he is smiling at me.

"Hello Cess, I'm here to collect you for the party," Showken says, looking around the room.

"I'm not going to your home. Look, you're a nice guy, you and your brothers, but Draken does not want me at the house, and I never go where I'm not wanted," I say, motioning for him to take a seat. I notice that he walks and sits very gracefully.

"My brother wants... never mind that, he is not home, Cess, and believe me, the last thing he will do is walk you off the property if you're there when he arrives," Showken says, looking at me curiously.

"I don't think that is happening, I mean who all is coming to the party?" I ask, not planning to go, but I just would like to know the list of invites.

"Oh it's really small, Cess. Come, let's go, you don't even need to change, you are dressed just right," he says, rising from the chair with his hand out.

"I didn't agree, Showken."

"Pleeeeeease," he begs, pouting. Yikes, he is fabulous and convincing. I guess I will go for just a little while. I smile, and rise, shaking my head. Why couldn't I say no to him?

"Okay, I'll go, but only for one hour."

"That's enough time," he says, and it sounds like there is a meaning behind that. He places his hand in mine, and we walk down the street to his house. I should not be going. We reach the house and he leads me down the side, towards the back. I've never been in this home before, from the outside it looks amazing.

"Showken, I didn't see any cars. Where is everybody?" I ask, still holding his hand. What is going on? This can't be a party. I hear music, but where are the people?

"Everyone is here, Cess, trust," he says, as we finally make it to the back yard. There is music playing, and food laid out as if a ton of people are coming. Yet I only see Gemi and Layern. That only makes four.

"I'm going home, I don't know what game you're playing, but I'm not that type of girl."

"Wait, I know what you are, and my brothers and I would like to show you we are fun. Last time we invited you, Draken asked you to leave, we are deeply sorry, that's all, Cess. We would never disrespect you. Never," he says, in a serious tone that makes me believe him.

"Okay, you don't have to go to all this trouble for me," I say, looking around, they have these beautiful colored drums around a circle.

"Yes, we do," Gemi says, coming up to me with a drink. I find myself blushing; this is way too much attention going on.

"Cess, we love to dance, like you, we are hoping you will dance, and we will play for you," Showken says. Layern is around the area with the drums. He has placed one in front of him as Gemi walks over to do the same.

"This is one way we say sorry, Cess, don't take this from us," Showken says, pulling me towards the center of these drums. I feel excited. I hear the drums as they begin to play, and my body just begins to move on its own.

"I do like to dance," I say, sipping my drink.

"That's the spirit Cess, feel the music." Layern says, smiling at me. I begin to dance, and forget they are even there. I can't believe they did all this for me. I feel the beat and let my body go, turning and twisting my body in all ways. I've been dancing for just a few minutes when the wind blows and I smell him, instantly stopping my dance.

"Hello, Cess," Draken says, moving closer to me. I can't move. He looks so sexy walking towards me. Everything south is wet. I feel like a fool. I can't keep my eyes off him as he approaches me. He stands a foot away, just looking at me, gliding his purple eyes over my body. My breasts instantly harden when we make eye contact. We stare at each other without speaking.

"I was invited," I say, finding my voice.

"Oh, well I like entertainment also, Cess, besides, remember, you owe me something," Draken says, coming closer. I feel the need to kiss him, like in my dream. I want him.

"I, I, umm, don't owe you," I say, feeling really hot now. I should go.

"You owe me, Cess, and I want a dance. I hear from my brothers you can dance. Now I want a private viewing of your... skills," he says, not stopping the eye contact.

"Draken, I'm sorry for coming to your home, I will leave now," I say, trying to get past him, but instantly I feel his hands on my waist, holding me in place.

"You will dance with my brothers, and not dance with me?

Why? I'm not as handsome as they are?" he asks, looking into my eyes, searching. I see the other brothers are not leaving this time. It's as if they are waiting for the answer to a question, more than just a dance.

"I thought you didn't want me at your house, now you want a dance?" I say, frowning a little.

"You have such bravery about you, Cess. Yes, I want you to dance for me, and then I will dance for you; if you don't like it, then you may leave," Draken says, with a small smile. Yikes, I could climax with that look he just gave me. Please don't let me go back on my promise.

"So, what's it going to be?" Showken says. I turn and see all eyes are on me. What are they waiting for?

"Fine, I'll do one dance," I say. Draken turns me around to face me, placing a very slow, tender kiss on my lips. Shit! I'm in freaking trouble.

"Cess, you taste really good," Draken says, and my dream comes rushing back to me. He couldn't know, could he? He goes and takes a seat near Gemi, and all of these men are staring at me like I'm a prize. I smile, hoping the drums will start, that will keep me focused. I need to hurry, before I end up in Draken's bed. That kiss he just gave me has lit a fire in my body that is getting hotter. How will I stay out of this man's bed? The tempo of the music they are playing begins to slow, and so does my body. I feel so special being here, as if it's an honor to dance for them. Taking a chance, I open my eyes, and see that Draken is in full eye contact with me. That dream keeps coming into my mind, his lips on mine. I remember a heat in my lower belly, and that feeling of great pleasure. His eyes are so beautiful, and I feel the blush coming. He must notice too, because I get the most perfect smile. I don't know if fighting this attraction is a good thing. Can Draken really be nice? His smile says that being with him could be nice, better than nice, fantastic. I can't dance any more, his eyes are so intense, running over my body very slowly. He uncrosses his legs, standing up, moving slowly, coming towards me, my mouth is open. I want him so bad, I start fidgeting, what is he going to do? I try to exit before he reaches me.

"Oh, I . . . need to, umm, go. Yeah, I need to go," I say, not moving from the spot.

"Really? I think you should stay," Draken says, reaching me. He stands so close, not touching, but wow, this heat I feel, and it's not because it's a hot night. This heat that I can't explain is getting hotter in my belly. He looks me straight in the eyes, not moving. I can't look away. What is he doing to me? My body is reacting to him in a way I've never experienced. I have never wanted someone this bad. I don't even know this guy. His chest is rising very slowly as he takes slow breaths in and out. I see his mouth move, but no words come out. What did he say?

"Umm, did you say something?" I ask, feeling like a horny mess.

"Yes, I was asking you to come inside," he says, smiling at me. Is he making fun of me? I never like that. He holds his hands near my face, not touching, but he is outlining it. He finally touches my hair, and that small touch makes a low moan escape my lips. "Mmm," it comes out again. I want his touch, it's almost a longing, as if I have had it before and miss it. He takes a step closer, and our faces are so close I feel his breath on my lips. He speaks right into my mouth.

"Can I kiss you? Please," Draken says, searching my eyes for a yes.

"Oh, okay," is all I can manage.

"Close your eyes, Cess. Just feel," he says. Without thinking I do it. I feel soft lips on mine and I think he is going to start kissing me, but he licks my lips very slowly, as if he is tasting me. I open my mouth just a little, and he assaults it. We are kissing, and I find the strength to reach and place my hands on his shoulders. I feel very warm hands meet my lower back, making a shiver go through my body. I can't get enough, and I feel him squeeze very tight around me. I feel like

I've fallen into the rabbit hole, never to return. I want to feel his beautiful long hair, and I run my hands through it. My body is submitting to him with no hesitation. He pulls back and my eyes open. "You are going to get me into trouble, Cess. Are you going to join me in my house?" he asks.

"Umm, Draken," I say, blushing. "This is moving really fast. I mean you were just telling me to stay off your property, and now, umm, now you want me?

"Why do you need an explanation? Can you just go with what you feel at this moment? I wanted you when I first met you, Cess. Do you want me?" he asks, rubbing my back very slowly. This is making it hard to make a good decision. He must feel my hesitation. "You worried about our not knowing each other, I tell you what, I will make sure we get to know each other, just say yes and come in so I can feel you."

"Whoa, you are so straightforward," I say, looking around for his brothers. They have all left. I wonder when that happened. I didn't see that happen. I can't sleep with him, it doesn't matter how bad I want him. I'm not a slut.

"Yes, I am to the point. I know what I want, and right now I would like you." He stares at me, waiting for me to answer.

"I, I, Draken," I say.

"Mmm, say it again," he says, licking his lips.

"Say what?" I ask, distracted by his lips.

"My name, say it again, I like the sound of it leaving that sweet mouth," he says, eyeing me intensely. I'm not sure if I can do this.

"Oh, Draken," I say, seeing his hand is out for me. If I take his hand, my gut is telling me things will never be the same. I don't know this man, but it feels so right being with him. I am about to place my hand in his, when I decide against it, pulling back. He cocks his head, looking at me like I should not have done that.

"Cess, hesitation is not something you should do. Follow your first mind. I just want to talk first."

"I don't know about this, Draken. I mean my last relationship was really hard on me, and I just can't put myself out to be hurt like that again," I say, fidgeting.

"Hmmm, I won't hurt you. Now can we go have a drink, and eat some dinner? I'm sure my brothers are eager to have you at the table," he says, taking my hand. Oh wow, I feel a heat go through me like a current. He just looks at me, searching again. I walk with him into his house, and it's beautiful. I mean the décor, for men, is spectacular.

The paintings look amazing. I've never seen such beautiful paintings before. They should be in a museum. I stop at one painting with a guy standing on a cliff. His face is not painted, but a purple dragon stands next to him as the sun is setting. They look close. Wow! I stop to get a closer look.

"Who painted this?" I say, wanting to touch, but not wanting to damage it.

"Someone I know painted this picture. Come, dinner is waiting," he says, and we finally make it to a dining room. It is all white. I mean, everything is white. I will not eat, I'm not sure why the room is white, it's really weird for men to have an all white room. I see his brothers smiling at me. Why are they so happy I'm here, this is weird. I turn to look at Draken, whose face is unreadable, but he is staring at me.

"We have never eaten with a lady before, Cess, at this table. We are honored you joined us. Please sit," Draken says, pulling a chair out next to the head chair.

"Okay, thank you. I am very happy to be here with you all. Thank you for inviting me," I say, sitting.

"I hope you like to eat, Cess, Showken and my brothers have prepared a feast for you," Draken says, smiling. Oh, there it goes again, the need to kiss him. I need a distraction.

"You guys don't have a cook?" I say.

"We are very private, Cess, and when we are here, we live very independently. At home, it's a different story," Showken says, winking at me.

"Oh." That is the only response I have. The table is decked out with roast lamb, some beef dish, and lots of fish of different sorts, with tons of veggies. They really can eat - this looks like it could feed about a hundred people. They all look very fit, so they must work out, to eat this way.

"What would you like to eat first, Cess," Gemi says, looking very handsome and sexy. Yikes, I should not be around so many men alone. I feel uncomfortable. I hope none of them are killers. That very moment, they all began to chuckle and shake their heads.

"I'm not real hungry, I'll take some lamb and veggies, please," I say, smiling.

"Save room for dessert," Draken says, handing me a plate that has been fixed very quickly by Layern. I guess he knew what I would want. I blush under Draken's comment, feeling so embarrassed.

"Cess, you are truly beautiful," Showken says, smiling.

"Showken, stop making Cess blush," Gemi says.

"Yes, let's eat," Draken says, commanding. The room falls silent. They all eat cautiously, not spilling a drop. I'm eating very cautiously in this all-white room, I've been in white rooms before, but this room is different, I can't put my finger on it, but it's too white, if there is such a thing. Who would have a dining room all white? I watch them all as they finish their plates, going back for seconds and thirds. Wow! They can put away some food. I can't eat that much, so I eat half my overloaded plate, finally pushing it away.

"Cess, you want dessert?" Showken says, and all the rest are staring at me. My, oh my, these are some very sexy men.

"Umm, no, I'm full."

"Great, Cess and I need to speak," Draken says, and with a nod to me, the brothers rise, leaving the room. Now I'm alone with him again. I turn and see him looking at me. Then he speaks.

"Cess, I would like you to be . . . would you date me?" Draken says. He speaks so calmly, yet his eyes are dancing, searching, full of hope.

"I, umm this is really, umm, why?" I ask. I need to know what he wants with me. I'm not the type he will need. My mouth is smart, I don't take orders, and I'm scared.

"I like you, Cess." Draken says, reaching to rub my hand. "For you spoke up to me which is rare, you are interesting to say the least, and to be honest, your body and smell make me want to explore your body, giving you a great deal of pleasure. Now before you reject, I'm here only for six months, so commitment is not a concern. I know you have a life you want. I just would like you to be mine while I'm in town. I know this sounds crazy to you, but to me, Cess, it sounds like a great adventure for you and me," Draken says, reaching to rub my hand. I feel that heat again. His touch is amazing.

"Well, let's be honest then," I say. "You say you want to date me for six months, with sex and no commitments. Why in the hell would I do that?" I ask, getting a little pissed.

"Cess, you want me like I want you," Draken says, stretching back in his chair. "We are two adults, although I am a little older, you're still an adult. I don't like fighting about what I know will happen. I think you should give me a chance to show you how good it can be. Will you let me?"

I do want this man, but this is really something out of my league. My dad says all the time: "Cess, in the business world, men can ask for anything." Draken just asked me to be a sex buddy for six months. I made a promise, and here I am about to break it. It's only for six months.

"Cess, I can see your confusion. Will you spend the night?"

Draken says, tilting his head. Holy shit! He just basically asked me to sleep with him. This is our first conversation really, the first time he just walked me off the property. This is not happening. It must be a dream. "Cess?" he calls. I'm shocked right now, but mostly hot. It's been a while since I've been with a man. I should do what Suzy says and have some fun. I mean, I don't want commitments right now in my life, maybe he could be my way to get over Travis.

"I'll stay, tonight, not guaranteeing anything. The six month commitment is too much to decide right now, but to be honest, I would love to have a one-night stand," I say, squaring my shoulders. He is not the only one who can say how he feels. Draken smiles.

"Cess, if you sleep with me tonight, you will sleep with me when I ask for the six months." Draken says, his unreadable face. "One-night stands are what you all made up. I don't believe in that. I have requested a time limit. You can accept or decline. I must say, I'm dying to get you in my bed, though,"

He is beautiful. I can see now that he is all about the man being in control. I just want to have some fun tonight, anything else sounds like a commitment. He stands and walks behind my chair, pulling it from the table. I feel myself getting excited. I'm really going to sleep with him. I have some condoms, and it's not like we are declaring ourselves a couple. People sleep with each other all the time for convenience.

"Okay," I say, as he grabs my hand and begins to walk me down a hall. This house is as big as ours. Oh, wow. This will most definitely be going in my Bio later in life. This is something I could write about.

DRAKEN

"Thank you for such vivid images of her desire, Layern," I say in my head, walking her to my room. I'm sure she is confused about my brothers' flirting, especially Showken. That will all end when I make her my Giver. The rule: no one can touch another Giver, or he will face a punishment given by the Taker. I can taste her again. The dream was just a taste. I can't wait to feel her. Her heart is beating so fast, I plan on making sure she enjoys herself.

"One night stand" she says, I will never have a Giver for one night. That is the problem with taking a human; they are so caught up with what's right with society. In my world, if you feel attraction to someone, in that instant sex can happen. Why deny yourself pleasure? Our women would never have given me trouble or questions. My brothers are intrigued about how I will deal with her in bed. I'll send some images, but just a few. I want her to myself. We finally walk into my room, and I know she is amazed about the bed. It has been brought especially from home. I feel my beast sensing her presence. I push it down. I have to protect her from my other aspect. I walk over to the bar, pouring her a drink to relax her more.

"Your room is very big," Cess says, walking around. She is intrigued with my material things. I just want her body now. I have to be gentle with her; don't want her dying on me the first time. I remove my shirt, and hear her gasp. She is the beautiful one, with those legs, and that smile is going to get me into trouble. I need her to be undressed. I walk over, hoping she doesn't back out.

"Yes, the room is big, but I don't want to talk about the room. Here is a drink, before I undress you," I say, admiring those breasts. In the dream, they were perfect, and now I get to touch them for real. This has been a long week, I can't wait to hear her scream.

"Thank you for the drink," she says, nervously.

"Trust me, I won't hurt you," I say. She takes a long gulp. I go and stand in front of her, listening to her precious heart. Hmm, I smell her sweetness. I need a taste. Taking her hand and heading for my bed, I stop her right in front of me. She starts to speak, but I need her to be quiet. Talking will make her think.

"Shh, no talking, our bodies will talk," I say, pushing her shirt up over her head. Her skin is so soft. She smells incredible. I'm removing her clothes slowly. I need her to know I don't want just me to feel pleasure. I will always please my Giver. Hmm, her legs are perfect. I hear her panting. Bending on my knees, I grab hold of her thighs and lick her calves. She almost falls as I place soft kisses on her inner thighs. "Uhhh," she moans. Yes, Cess, I like to hear you. I lay her down on my bed. She is squirming as she watches me undress.

"Draken, you have a tattoo? I would never have guessed," she says, panting. I have an effect on her. Feeling the nudge of my brothers wanting to see, I change my mind. I'm not sharing her image. She is too precious.

"Our bodies will talk, ask me questions later," I say. Moving back to those legs, I let the heat come through my hands as I massage her thighs, moving slowly towards her sex. I spread her legs, and she is wet for me. I hear the low growl within me. I continue the massage on her inner thighs, making sure she is relaxed. I graze one finger over her clitoris. Her cry is amazing. I have to stretch her.

"Wait, do you have condoms? I do."

"Cess, please follow directions and enjoy my gift to you, before you give." I say. I know how to stop all this conversation. I insert one finger, moving in . . . out . . . in . . . out. I do this at a very slow pace. I insert another finger, at the same pace. She is so wet it's like a sponge being squeezed. "Draken, please," she begs. I like sex talk.

"Please, what?" She pushes her pelvis towards my hand, trying to get me to go faster. No, I need her really open before I'm inside her.

"Draken." All I hear is panting.

"Say my name."

"DRAKEN!" she yells.

I continue my assault on her. I begin to pick up the speed, giving her an orgasm. Her sex clenches around my fingers as she screams. She is going to be fun. I feel very comfortable with Cess; this human woman is doing things to me inside that I've never felt. I'm so fucking hard right now. I can't, she's not ready. I don't want her to rip, then I would have to wait. Placing my mouth on those breasts, I suck and lick, grazing my teeth over her nipples. She starts pushing again, against my hand. I continue the slow pace, in . . . out . . . in . . . out. I know she wants me to go faster, but not yet. As I watch her enjoy me, my body reacts to her pleasure and moans. I've never felt the need to please anyone as much as Cess. I may not be able to let her go. I feel the nudge again from Showken, for access to see her. This beauty is too private. Her body is mine. I respond loudly in my head to Showken, "BACK OFF!" I feel the pull leaving, and focus back on this beautiful human. She has beautiful long brown hair. I notice her eyes are squeezed tight shut.

"You are so beautiful." I say, pushing my tongue into her

mouth. I release a heat again, giving her a feeling that she has never experienced. Her moans are so precious, giving me all I need to get ready for my taking. I may never let her go. A Giver is a Giver as long as the Taker wants. Looking at her, I realize six months may not be enough for me. I stand and remove my pants. She is looking at me with eyes of lust, hunger, and curiosity. With a low growl I try to suppress, I climb back into bed to finish the night.

CESS

Everything I've been taught about holding out on sex has gone down the drain. I have never had a man lick my calves and legs the way Draken is doing. I can't control my body. It has a mind of its own. I need to touch him. He's devouring me, and it feels like heaven. I find myself pulling at his purple sheets. I couldn't stop even if I wanted to. This is going to be the best one night stand ever. He is such a gentle lover. I can't believe he gave me a massage that made me orgasm.

My thoughts are everywhere right now- if he asked me to say I love you, I would. Oh my, he's undressing. His body is - ohh shit, he dropped his pants. He is not real, everything on his body is so perfect. Oh his abs, I really have to touch them. Oh wow, he is huge, extremely huge, that's going to hurt, and feel good. I can't control my moans. His hands are everywhere on my body.

"Hmm," is the only sound I can manage, gazing at him. Wait, he is naked without a condom. I'm not getting pregnant or catching an STD. "Draken, umm we, oh, need condom." I sound so stupid.

"You worry too much, I will not get you pregnant," Draken smiles, bending down and pulling my right breast into his mouth, sucking, pulling, grazing his teeth over my nipple making it harden. While he's squeezing my breasts, they become very sensitive. The heat is so intense, how does he do it? His fingers find my sex and he begins his torture, he pushes in, twisting his fingers. This feels so good. I think he has three fingers in me. Oh wow, he has me wide open without notice. I feel him push at my sex. "OOOOHHH!" I scream, feeling a little embarrassed, knowing his brothers are in the house. I know this house is big, but so is my mouth. I can't stop the screaming.

"Louder, Cess, let me hear you," he says, holding my legs apart. I'm no virgin, but Draken is huge. He must be taking something to be this large. Oh, damn, here I go again. He doesn't have on a condom, I don't want him to stop, flesh on flesh is always better. Please don't let me get pregnant or get an STD.

"DRAKEN!" I yell, again, panting. I need a break. I know he said all night, but really, all night screaming? I'm going to lose my voice.

"You look gorgeous screaming my name, Cess, I'm going to

stir it," he whispers. "Stir it like coffee, giving you more orgasms than you have had in your entire life," he says, in between kissing me and pushing farther inside. Oh my, he is still not completely in, I'm going to lose it. My body is shaking, and every time I think I can regain my thoughts, he continues.

"Please, I need a break," I say, still pushing forward. My mind is thinking one way and my body is asking for more.

"Shhh, hush and stop thinking. Your body wants more, now take a big breath in and blow out," he murmurs in my ear. I do it, not knowing what is coming, until I feel him push completely inside me. "ARGHHH!" I hold my breath, hoping the pain will go away. I'm all the way filled. He is huge. It hurts.

"Cess, look at me," he says, placing his hands on my face. I look into his eyes, and they have changed to dark purple. I guess he is really excited, like me. His hands are calming, the gentle strokes down my face help. I close my eyes, trying to relax. He has not moved, he is waiting for me to relax. He begins to rub my hip in circular movements. I feel myself relaxing, as he is saying all the right things.

"You are so beautiful, thank you for giving me this honor of pleasing you. You feel so good, baby. I love how you say my name, it's the best sound ever. I need you, just relax. I'm going to make you feel so good, baby, I want you to pull your legs up for me. Can you do that?" he asks. I'm panting from all these words and kisses. I begin to lift my legs, while he continues to rub my hip. As my legs get higher, it starts to feel better, and I slowly start to move. I feel him start a slow, circular movement. Oh, that feels amazing. He rests his head on my chest. His breathing is picking up. It is hot and teasing against my skin. I'm on fire inside, but it's a good feeling. I want to run, jump and scream all at once. This feeling is amazing. He starts to go faster, and my legs are getting weak. He must've felt them getting relaxed, because he places both hands under my thighs, right below my buttocks. Oh wow, he gives a good squeeze and then really takes off. I'm sweating, panting, screaming and moaning, not knowing what to do. I rub my hand over his tattoo and it's extremely hot, and when I remove my hand from that spot on his chest, my hand continues to burn. I bite my lip and he starts a counter-clockwise motion, slowing down. I'm going to pass out, it's coming, I can't keep at this. He's like a machine.

"Come on baby, stay with me, I promised you all night."

"I . . . can't . . . feels . . . oh . . . please . . . Draken!"

"Yes, you can. Just a little more and I'll let you rest for a while, before we start again."

"Huh?"

"Yes, all night, remember?"

"I'm screaming . . . brothers."

"Don't worry, I have the room protected."

I try to stay focused, but his assault is too much. I come hard and loud, and mumble as I slide into sleep. Draken wakes me in no time, and starts all over again. We go all night, and by the time he finally releases, I'm used to him being inside. What have I got myself into with this man?

"Sleep, Cess, you will need your rest for next time," Draken says, pulling me into his warm body. I notice he's not sweating, just me. I must feel like I just stepped out of a sauna to him. It doesn't seem to bother him. I'm too tired to go home, I fall asleep in his arms, smiling.

***

I feel so sore everywhere. I'm yearning, everything starts rushing back to me. I'm at Draken's house. I danced, ate- yikes, I slept with him! Well, not really slept. I'm in his bed, naked. I inhale deeply and can smell sex, Draken, and a beautiful smell coming from the bathroom. That's when I notice him humming in the shower. Oh, I spent the night. It's morning. Hurrying out of the bed I look for my clothes, thinking they should be on the floor. Where are my clothes? The bathroom door opens and he walks out. We stare at each other for a long time without speaking. He is wrapped in a towel that is almost like a beautiful wrap. He has it tied around his waist, and it is trimmed in gold. His taste is very elegant. Purple must be his favorite color. He continues staring. Feeling self-conscious about last night, I lower my head.

"Do you know where my clothes are?" I ask, softly. I

shouldn't have done this, I move a little and my body reacts with a shot of pain. This staring at me has to stop, I feel myself getting warm inside for this man. I need a hot bath and my own home.

"I folded your clothes and placed them on my dresser. I had Showken get you some fresh clothes from your home. I know you would like a bath, right?" Draken asks. He looks amazing. I didn't even get to do anything during sex but scream and moan. I should have been more active, maybe next time. Oh wait, not going to be a next time, remember, one night stand. How did he get me new clothes? Where do my parents think I am? I'm grown up, but not when it comes to Dad. My dad is not understanding about me staying out all night. I feel my face go from calm to the horror of my dad knowing I'm in bed with the neighbor; this is not a good look.

"Cess, remain calm," Draken says, coming to sit on the bed next to me, "I would never shame you, so relax. Showken got you some clothes without being seen, don't ask how, and your family thinks you decided to visit Kelly for the night." Oh, he smells so good. What did he say again? I spent the night with Kelly, Showken broke into my house . . . These are some crazy brothers. He is examining me, like he is scanning for bruises or marks.

"Umm, Draken," I say, looking down, "last night was, it was amazing, but I can't do this, this thing that you want. I will get my clothes and go home. Thank you, for covering for me so my dad won't freak out. I mean, I turn 21 in a couple of months, I hope

86

you understand." I can't meet his face, but as I'm talking, I hear a low growl, and I assume he is angry. The room starts closing in, and for the first time since I've been in his presence, I feel fear. What have I gotten myself into? He could be a killer. He takes a couple of deep breaths and relaxes. I hope he is not angry. What the hell was I thinking? I should have said something when I was home and safe.

Draken responds, "Cess, I will run your bath water for you, your fresh clothes are already in the bathroom. I have all the things you use daily, body wash, deodorant, lotion, hair products, perfume, even some jewelry that you might like to wear, but make no mistake, last night was just the beginning. I only understand that you feel good to me, making me want more of you. I hated to shower, because I wanted your smell on me all day. Please, do not wound me and stop this before we begin, try it and see. I can be okay. I will pick you up for dinner tonight, say around 7:00pm." He leans over, giving me a very passionate kiss. Oh, I feel the heat rising, and I want this man again. Fear is no longer present, just a need for him. He rises from the bed, heads to the bathroom, and starts running a bath. He must know I'm sore from all of his attacks. I'm in shock; he basically ignored my speech, and took it upon himself to do what he wanted. He is an alpha male, I can see that. I sit watching him as he moves about in the bathroom. He lights some candles and heads back to the room. He comes and stands next to the bed, smiling. He pulls very gently at the sheet, and I release it. Oh, what this man does to me.

"I know you're sore, I put something in the water to help with that," he says, leaning over and picking me up in a cradle position. My body responds, my nipples hardening with just his touch. He leans down and sucks my breast, I'm moaning into his chest. I just tried to stop this; he is way too skilled for me to stop him. "Mmm," is my response to this very intense feeling. I'm so caught up with his kissing and sucking, I don't notice we are in his bathroom. It's absolutely gorgeous. Fit for a king. WOW! He gently lowers me into the water, and I instantly grab him tighter.

"Oh, this is hot, and my special place is stinging," I say.

"It will only sting for a second, Cess, it will feel good," he says, placing another kiss on my neck. He stares at me, and I nod with my mouth closed tight, and boy does it sting. I grit my teeth and hold my breath. Within a couple of seconds, all the pain is gone.

"Thank you, Draken. You were right; it feels very good to me. What did you put in the water, it's very relaxing and smells so good?"

"It's an old family remedy that I can't reveal. Relax, the candles are from my home, and they will help you relax as well. I'll see you later, take your time and have no worries, the water will remain hot for you," Draken says, turning to leave. When the door is closed, I smile hugely. My body feels so good in this water. I'm so relaxed. I lean back and enjoy. Draken can be kind, yet I know he has a mean side. I've seen it. I'm already spoiled, and Draken is adding to this by carrying me to the bathroom, lighting candles and giving me so many orgasms. Just thinking about last night, I feel the blush rising. I may never want to leave. Let me get my head right; what does he want me to be like? I'm not sure what he wants, besides sex, he never said. I need to find out more about him, and that low growl he does is scary as hell. I'm not sure how he can even do that, it sounds like an animal. I will talk with him later. Now, I will enjoy this wonderful bath that's been prepared for me.

DRAKEN

Getting dressed in some casual clothes, I head out of the room.
She is not going to stop being my Giver until I say so, not a second
before. I walk to the study where my brothers are waiting. Hawken
is here, staring at me as if I've committed a crime. (Hawken is one
of my brothers, and we don't get along with each other, it's been
this way for as long as I can remember.) He storms right up to me,
and before I know it, I have slammed him to the ground, punching
his face, ribs and back. He jumps on my back and wraps his arm
around my neck, choking me.

My other brothers don't move, it's not what we do. If one
brother is fighting, the others are not allowed to interfere, even if a
death occurs. Only our father can stop us. I pull him over my

shoulder, releasing a roar. I'm glad Cess can't hear this. Thanks to the remedy, she thinks it's quiet. I release fire from my mouth, causing him to fly across the room, severely burned. It will take him a few days to heal.

"What the fuck is your problem, coming here, Hawken?" I ask, looking at him and wondering if I should hit him again with a burn.

"You have jeopardized our land with your human," Hawken says, with clenched teeth. He rises and stands, not taking his eyes off me. This is my most dangerous brother.

"What are you talking about?" I yell. Showken stands and holds his hands up in surrender. He then begins to speak.

"Okay, apparently, the laws state that when an heir to the throne takes a Giver that is human, and falls in love, she has to be his mate. Well, since we are dragons, not sure how she's going to feel when she sees your true form. Sorry, shit happens," Showken says, stepping back.

"Father wants you home now, to speak with you. Do you know that our land will be tainted if our fucking heir marries a human? It will be chaos," Hawken snaps, gaining his strength by the second.

"I will confirm this with Father later," I say, glaring at Hawken, "right now I have company. I'll come home tomorrow."

"You will come now, Father says you must come now! Showken will watch your fucking mate, you asshole!" Hawken snarls. I let out another hit of flames on him, bringing him to his knees.

"I have no problem with killing you," I say, "so watch your mouth. I will come to see Father, not because you say so, only out of respect for Father. But, if you disrespect me one more time, we will be short one brother, do you understand me?" I slide my hand into my pocket, opening the emergency portal to my home, Cortamagen. Fuck, Cess is going to think I have left her. I hope Showken does something, I like her. I'm not in love with her, though. I will clear this up and get back to Cess.

***

I walk through the castle, my home. Seeing the beauty of it brings a yearning to come home. Passing the staff, I'm greeted numerous times as "Prince Draken, heir to our Kingdom." I continue my walk, not speaking, just wanting to see what is going on. I stop trying to sniff and smell my father, the King of Cortamagen. I suddenly catch the smell of my mother, and know she will be close by. I find her in the garden, eating fruit. I bow as she turns and sees me.

"Queen Nala, Mother of Draglen descendants, I humbly request permission to speak," I say, remaining in my bowing position. Though this is my mother, whom I love dearly, in Cortamagen tradition is everything. I usually greet her in this manner, and then I will be granted permission to speak.

"Of course, my son. Come. Sit. Tell me why you have fallen for this human. Speak freely, my eldest," Queen Nala says, patting the spot on the bench next to her. I swallow hard, not knowing what to say. I don't love Cess. I enjoy her as a Giver, nothing more.

"Mother, I'm confused. I'm not in love with anyone, yet I'm being accused of bringing disgrace to our land. I would never do that. I would burn a thousand times before I would. Who has made this accusation against me?" I ask, looking into my mother's eyes. With her hair, red as a flame and her eyes, bright and clear as a star, she is more beautiful than any in our land. She gently reaches for my face, placing her hand on my cheek, she looks sad.

"My son, my Draken, my firstborn," my mother says, "your accuser am I, the seer of this land. You will fall for this Cess, soon wanting her as your mate, and she will want you. My son, I would be happy if she were not human, yet the truth is, she is, and she can't come to our land. Your father is very upset. He went flying, and should be back shortly. My son, you are engaged already, to Velca. She is perfect for you, ready to bring forth more sons for our family, our kingdom; this human will taint our blood, transforming us into something we know nothing about." Taking a breath, she releases me. "Now, you tell your father you will not see her again, and this can be just a bad dream." My mother is the seer, and has never been wrong. I don't feel anything for Cess. She is just a Giver. I would not marry a human.

"Mother, I made her my Giver, she pleases me, I don't want to stop," I say. This is not happening, I knew that Cess would be trouble. I'm not done with her, and I surely will not give her up. My other brothers have taken human woman many times, on Earth. I can, too. "Mother, it's not fair to ask me to release my Giver, my brothers have never been asked such a thing," I snap. Her head turns quickly towards me, and I know I've been too aggressive with my tone. I bow my head in apology for speaking harshly.

"My son, watch your tone with me, I'm not afraid, remember that," she says. "She is your Giver now, but you already defend her, you speak as if you can't have another human Giver. Besides, you have Ravla, she is more than capable of pleasing you."

Feeling hopeless and pissed all at once, I search my heart, thinking, do I really want this Cess? She does make me feel better than any Giver I've had, and not feeling that again is not an option. There has to be another way, other than stopping seeing her. My animal wants out. I feel the need to be released into my beast.

"Forgive me, Mother, I do not ever wish to upset you," I say. She turns and looks at me.

"You need to fly, my son, your eyes are such a dark purple right now. I believe you will understand better after you fly, now go, and release your beast," she smiles, taking another piece of fruit. I stand and walk toward the center of the garden, a safe place to change without destroying the castle. I feel the burn and need to turn, to release my beast. My body transforms, stretching, widening. I'm forced to the ground, where my head gets bigger. I lift my head and see my mother smiling, with all the pride a mother should have for her child. In no time I'm transformed into my beast. I spread my wings and roar in the air.

I bow at my mother, and she says, "Go, my son, fly and enjoy yourself." With that, I'm in the air at high speed, flying over the mountains and under the sacred tombs. I can't believe I'm being forced to release a Giver. My father is more than likely flying, so he won't try killing me for having such strong feelings for a human. I fly until I come to my favorite place to think, the Great Jewel Cliff. I stand, thinking. Could Mother be wrong? She has never been wrong. There must be some truth to what she says, because I can't wait to get back to Cess and be with her. Could I fall in love with her? I do know releasing her is not going to happen any time soon. This is my first human, and I still want to play. I've never had a human, and why are they so sure it's her, it could be someone else. I guess I should head back. I turn, flying back to the castle, enjoying my flight, and suddenly I feel a pull from someone. It's not from my family. It's Cess. She is yearning for me. I must get home, fast. I make my way back to the garden, where my mother and father are sitting. I transform back to human form, grabbing a wrap, as our clothes are always in shreds after transformation. I walk towards my parents. I bow, showing my father the same respect as my mother, when I'm hit again with need for Cess. I need to get home.

"King Dramen, Ruler of Cortamagen, Father of Draglen Descendants, I request to speak," I say, feeling an urgency to get back to Cess. I hope Showken's taking good care of her. I don't want her leaving for home just yet.

"You can speak, my son, only if you are saying what my Queen has told me," my father says, piercing me with his stare. I glance at my mother, who is glaring at me. If I say I will not see her again, it will be a lie that will result in some form of punishment, which would include the death of Cess. I want to see her again. In fact, my body aches to get home to be inside her. I bow my head, showing respect to my father, while in deep thought, trying to figure out the words to say, abruptly I hear my father's voice speaking a word in our old language.

"CATI!" he yells, standing. I've just been called a fool. I glance up, meeting my father's eyes with a stare. I will not back down, if I want her as a Giver, I will have her. "You will stop this disgrace."

"I will return to earth," I say, letting him and my mother know I'm not backing down.

"My son, please, you are to be married in six months. This Cess I see is interfering with our world. Choose another human if you must have one, but not her, she will pierce your heart," my mother pleads. My father glares at her as if she's said something wrong.

"The law states, any descendant of Draglen blood may choose his Giver without interference from another. I choose Cess. Now that we have that settled, I'm going back to Earth, to lie with my Giver," I say, snapping each word out of my mouth.

"Your bride? Ravla?" my mother asks. My father is just watching me. I can only assume if I had not been his son, I would be dead right at this moment. He turns and walks back into the castle, and everyone can sense his mood. He speaks, in old language, cursing me. I glare at his back and turn to look at my mother, now looking saddened. "I see. You will change our land, Draken. Please reconsider."

"I will marry my bride, and Ravla is still my Giver. I just don't need her at this time. I choose Cess, and Cess I will have," I say, going over to the bench and pressing a gentle a gentle kiss on my mother's hand. She holds her hand and rubs my head. "My son, always so determined. Look, I have a portal waiting for you," she says. I turn around and there is a portal back to earth waiting. I look into her eyes.

"I will return in six months to marry," I say, walking to the portal. My need for Cess is becoming painful.

As I walk through the portal, I hear my mother say "With whom will you marry, is the question." The portal closes as I make my way back to Cess. I need her badly.

CESS

That was the best bath ever. I feel so refreshed. Yet I'm hungry, as well. I'm so afraid to leave this room. I know his brothers heard my screaming. This is going to be embarrassing. Oh well, it happens.

Draken is a wonderful lover, and I might want to have another round. One-night stands do not even seem logical for a man who can make you scream like that. I find my clothes in the bathroom, like he said. He had them bring me a summer dress. It's a light purple one that ties around my neck, with a split up to my thigh on the left side. This dress is one of my favorites. I put on all my lotion and girly things, and slip into my dress, noticing a pair of shoes to match. Those are not mine. Why did he give me these shoes? Are they for me? I'm not going to risk it, they may be some other woman's. I hate even thinking about someone else receiving all that Draken can bring to the bed. I think he was holding back on me, too, and I'm glad. I take a deep breath and open the door to his room. There is a beautiful man standing there waiting. He scares me and I yell.

"Ahhh!" I yell, in a state of shock. He just stands there and smiles. Oh my, he is just as handsome as the others. He is beautiful. He must be related somehow to the others, they all share that gorgeous smile. I stop screaming, and we just stare at each other. He is about 6'5", with light brown hair. His eyes are light brown, as well. He finally speaks.

"I see why my brother wants you, Cess. You are beautiful," he says. I begin walking backwards, going back into Draken's room.

"You're Draken's brother, I didn't meet you," I say, remembering my defense classes. This guy looks really scary.

"Oh, I just came into town. Now, breakfast is waiting for you. Come, let's go eat, as the others are waiting," he says, turning to leave without giving me his name. What kind of family is this?

"What is your name?" I ask, watching him walk away.

"Hawken is my name, but you can call me Hawk," he says, stopping. "Come, Cess, we are all hungry, and you're holding us up from eating," he snaps. Shit, they can eat without me. Why didn't Draken come and get me himself? You are not allowed to have sex with me and leave your brother to come fetch me like a pet. I'm leaving. I feel Hawk pulling me down the hall. "I see you're not good at taking orders, if you plan on "dating" my brother, orders you will be given, and orders you will take," Hawk says, walking me quickly to the white dining room. Showken, Gemi, and Layern are all sitting waiting, I assume for me.

"Yes, she is here, now, let's eat," Gemi says, and begins to dig into a very lavish breakfast. It's just Saturday, not a special occasion, yet the food laid out is in huge amounts. Why do they eat so much? And where the hell is Draken? Why is he not at the table?

"Draken had to make a run, Cess, he will be joining us soon," Layern says, to my unspoken concern. Layern has such pain behind his eyes. I never noticed it before, but he seems sad, lost even. I wonder why?

"Why don't you wait for him? You waited for me," I say, still standing. I'm not sure about being here with all of these sexy, good-looking men. I notice Showken's huge smile, and relax instantly. He knows how to make you feel comfortable.

"We always wait for the lady in the house, Cess. Please, come sit and eat," Showken says, waving his hand for me to sit across from him. I go and sit, and he fixes my plate for me. These men take my breath away with all this attention. I could get used to this.

"Thank you for fixing my plate," I say, grabbing a fork and eating the eggs. They are so good. All this food, if I eat with them I'm going to be huge. We eat in silence a few minutes, before

Hawk speaks.

"So, Cess, I would love to know how you - I mean, I would love to know about you," Hawken says.

"Well, umm, Hawken. I don't have much to say about myself, except, I'm very wealthy, the first daughter and granddaughter to some very powerful men. Perhaps you have heard of my family name, Lamil?" I say, with a glare. I don't like Hawken, and he doesn't like me either. If using my family name gets him to think twice about upsetting me, then I will.

"As a matter of fact, I have heard of Lamil. Powerful, you say they are?" He smirks. What is it with him? I put on my best smile and continue to eat. I can't wait until Draken comes back from his run.

"Hawken, enough," Layern says, and I notice them all staring at him. He smiles, and yikes, he is gorgeous too. This gene pool of brothers is unreal. How many brothers are there, I wonder?

"Cess, I apologize for my mouth, it gets me into trouble often. I would hate such a beautiful lady as yourself to be angry with me. Do you accept my apology?" Hawken asks.

"You're fine, Hawken, there is no harm done," I say, wondering is it my name that made him squirm, or the looks from his brothers.

We eat the rest of the meal in silence. I can't eat much, as I continue to think about my night with Draken. "Umm", I moan out loud, "Hmmm," closing my eyes. I open one eye and notice everyone is staring at me. Damn, I didn't mean to do that out loud. Everyone is staring at me, with smiles and smirks.

"Have a good night, Cess?" Showken asks, taking a huge forkful of food.

"Umm, yes. I slept well," I say, blushing.

"You were in my brother's room all night, Cess, sleep is not what you got, I'm sure," Showken says, laughing and stuffing his mouth with more food.

"Huh?"

"Huh, Cess, we all know our brother and you were in his bed last night," Hawken says, stuffing food in his mouth, too. They all eat as much as twenty men.

"Well, umm, can we change the subject, please?" I say feeling the blush over my face again. I really wish you were here now, Draken, your brothers would behave for you. Just as I have that thought Draken walks in, looking fabulous, I want him.

"Stop asking questions," he says, heading straight for me. His brothers continue eating. "Hello, Cess. Please forgive me for not being here when you came out for breakfast. Were my brothers good?" he asks, sitting down at the head of table, not taking his eyes off me. Oh, this man has me warming up inside. I glance at Hawken, who is the only one who's been rude to me. As I am about to speak, Draken leans in and sniffs me. Holy crap! What's that about?

"Hawken, why did you touch her?" he asks, narrowing his

eyes.

"Whoa, yeah, umm, brothers, we have company at the table, lets discuss this later," Showken says. Hawken and Draken are having a stare down.

"It's not what you think, but I agree with Showken, later is better," Hawken snaps.

"Later," Draken says, with a promise.

"I should head home," I say, getting ready to leave. His hand touches my thigh. Oh God, he looks amazing. He looks at me silently, and I decide maybe a little longer is not so bad.

"Thank you," Draken whispers, rubbing my thigh in a very slow circle, like he was doing last night. I know leaving is not an option right now. I catch the flicker of his eye color from light to dark purple. Never seen that before, but I've never seen a group of brothers like this, either.

"You're welcome," I say, in a whisper. I feel myself blushing, so I know all these hot men can see it. Draken is staring at me like he wants me right this moment. Frankly, being with him again sounds good. I know D is wondering where I'm at, unlike my parents, who will think that I'm at Kelly's. D already knows I'm not there. D and I have a very strong bond. We are twins, but he is my best friend too, and he will never tell, but the interrogation when I get home is going to be annoying. I might as well have fun before my brother brings logic to me and says, "Cess, you don't need to be seriously involved with someone right now, if you were a guy, I would say get all you can, but you're not." I hear his voice clearly; just thinking about it, I smile to myself. I glance over at Draken, and he's watching my every move. Yikes, he looks like an angel. There goes my promise.

DRAKEN

Hawken better keep his claws off Cess, before I rip them out.
He knows the rules, no touching another's Giver unless permission
is granted by the Taker.

Walking in and seeing Cess eases my worries for just a
moment. Purple looks good on her, I must thank Showken for
picking the right attire. Forcing myself to eat, ignoring her beauty,
I can tell her mind is wandering. I love her eye movement as she is
thinking, with those beautiful milk-chocolate eyes, searching.
Breakfast is not moving fast enough. I'm sure my emergency trip
home has all of my brothers worried. I'm not in love with Cess, but
I'm not letting her go until I'm ready, not because I'm told.

"What information did you find out on your run?" Layern

asks, narrowing his eyes. I have been thinking of everything except what I was told back home. That question rushes everything back.

"Everything is fine," I say, glaring at Hawken. His smirk is really pissing me off. "Anything funny, Hawken?" I ask.

"Why, yes, there is my oldest brother. I have my doubts about the situation at hand. I mean, it's funny when you know the truth and still lie to yourself," Hawken says, shaking his head.

"If you two don't behave like there's a lady at the table, the consequences for not complying will be bad, so just stop this," Gemi says, running his hand through his hair. I'm done with this, six months is what I have, and then I marry. This conversation ends now. Glaring at Layern, I let him know telepathically to let my brothers understand my feeling on this issue with Cess. My patience with this topic has grown thin.

"I'm done. Cess, have you eaten enough?" I ask, looking at her now curious face. This is what I'm trying to avoid. Human women know nothing about Givers, and will take it as an insult, when, in fact, many women in Cortamagen would love this title. I feel her hesitation, so I lean down, giving her a gentle kiss to reassure her everything is fine. It's just what she needs. She gave me her precious smile, and all my anger slips away.

"Yes, I can't eat another bite," Cess says, "I was wondering if I could see the rest of your house. It's very beautiful, and the art in here is museum-worthy." Damn, I just want to lick her thighs, belly, and oh yes, that sweet treasure. I wish she knew the Givers' rules, and then I could march her into my room for a day or two.

"If you want a tour of the house, then let's get started, we have a lot of ground to cover," I say, holding out my hand to her. Feeling the soft hand she places in mine is amazing, knowing it's like a feather to me, so easily broken if I choose. Yet it could make me feel really good if this feather is rubbed the right way.

We start our walk down the expansive hall, which has many portraits of my family in both human and dragon form. There is also a picture of our castle. Its history goes back thousands of years. We are always allowed to take this to Earth to keep us grounded, and besides, legend has it that the paintings can come to life.

"Draken, this is so beautiful, who painted these portraits?" Cess asks, gazing at the pictures. It's really nice to meet someone who likes history. Although she thinks it's just a painting, it's much more.

"These paintings are painted by close friends of the family," I say, trying not to expose our identity. I really would like to make her scream again. I place my hands behind my back and walk slowly, calming my dragon. This getting to know me is not what I expected, I just want some pleasure.

"Please don't get offended by this, Draken, but why is everything a reference to dragons in this hall? Does your family have an obsession with dragons? I mean, you don't actually believe in them, do you?" she asks, with a playful grin.

"How can I answer this, hmm, my family and I very much respect the dragon. Many have tried to make them out to be bad, when actually, they are more than likely just like you," I say, not moving my eyes, feeling my beast surface and knowing my eyes are dark purple as my dragon needs her body. I should be offended by her comment, but it's not her fault her planet decided that making dragons bad and mythical was more beneficial. I wonder what their belief in their precious dinosaurs came from? Dinosaurs are merely pets, which got out of control on earth. Now, they walk freely on Cortamagen. I see her curiosity has only gotten worse.

Fuck! I need her in my bed. I lean in, whispering in her ear. "Can I please you, and we can talk about it another day?" I lick the back of her neck, wrapping my hands around her waist. Smelling her arousal, feeling her clench her legs tight, just makes me want her more. I need her in my room, fast. I rub my hand over her breast, feeling the hardness of her nipple, not stopping my licking of her neck and shoulder, making sure to get her as hot as possible. This talk of dragons is dangerous. Especially since she is about to have sex with one again.

"Ah, mmm, Draken, that feels so good," she moans, very softly.

"Cess, I want you to understand, you're mine, and no other man is allowed to touch you, or you to touch him unless he is family. I questioned the family thing, since your land is big on family sex," I say, really wishing I could have worded that better. I

108

meant every word. Just now, I see anger on Cess' face. I have to fix this quick. "What I'm trying to say is, before you get angry," I say, "I just don't like to share. When I'm with a woman I want her to myself. I'm very selfish. I should have said it like that. Yet, I still mean every word. I'm jealous, Cess, and if another man touches you, or I sense him coming on to you, my actions will not be controlled." I hope that will help.

"Draken, I'm an adult and I do as I please. My father's name is Don, not Draken, remember that," Cess says, pushing away and continuing to admire the paintings. I think I should wait a few minutes, giving her time to cool down. This is why I didn't want a human female, I'm heir to our throne, and she has me apologizing to her, my Giver. This is going to be different.

"Cess, I don't want to argue with you," I say. I lean in to smell her hair, and its scent is intoxicating. "I would like to make you climax a few times, if you don't mind," I say, sweeping her hair to the left shoulder so I can give soft kisses to her back. Her body shivers, and that gives me an idea. Wrapping my arms around her waist, I pull her really close, so she can feel my erection. I begin a slow rub on her lower abdomen, and can feel her arousal, her wanting of me. She is willing, and waiting for my touch. Sliding my hand over her sex, I cup her through the dress, pressing hard. This is what I want - my Giver to be willing when I say.

"Draken, umm, we could be seen, please, I, whoa, yes," Cess says, barely getting the words out. I don't listen to her, I watch her body move in a slow wave, with my hand on that very wet pleasure she is having. I want her to get used to me. I continue my assault, squeezing her breast, feeling the softness and the now hardening nipple. Yes, she is going to be a great Giver. We need to move to my room. I turn her slowly, my hands cupping her face. I place a very strong kiss on those lips, my lips. Her body belongs to me.

"Cess, come. Let's go back to bed for a while," I say, looking her up and down. I'm going to burst. Quieting my beast is becoming a task around Cess.

"Draken," Cess says, pushing away from me. "As much as I would like to go climb back in bed with you, I can't. I need to go home and clear my head. Breaking promises is bad enough in my book, but it's even worse when you break a promise to yourself. I like you. Oh, heaven knows I do, but I must go home," I can feel her heartbeat, and it's going very fast. She doesn't want to leave; she's fidgeting, smiling. I place my hands together, letting them rest over my erection. I look her up and down, not saying a word. I need her right now, but I will let her go home this time.

"I don't want you to go, but if you must leave, may I have something?" I ask, looking for any sign of resistance.

"Uh, sure," Cess says, with wonder in those beautiful eyes. I walk slowly up close to her, and drop to my knees. Looking up at her, I push her dress up until it is around her waist, and I can see yellow lace panties. Holding her dress in a bunch with one hand, and sliding down her panties with the other, I begin to have my dessert. If she is going home, I'm getting something. She is delicious, better than any food I've ever eaten. Doing slow to fast licks between her folds, I feel her legs going weak, so I let go of her dress and grab her thighs, holding her up. It is not long before she is screaming, and I'm getting my fill licking and sucking, and she reaches her climax, not stopping until I'm done.

When I finish, pulling her panties back up and straightening her dress, I rise in front of her, giving her a kiss. She doesn't know I saved her some dessert, too. She should know how good she tastes, so when she opens her mouth, I kiss her hard, pushing some of her sweet juice into her mouth. She loves it, her moans are my weakness.

"Thank you, Cess, for dessert," I say, licking my lips.

"Yes, well, thank you, also," Cess, says, with a lustful look. Yes, my sweet Giver, think really hard when you go home. Soon you will be my Giver.

"Every time, my Cess. Every. Single. Time," I say, grabbing her hand to walk her home. Her intake of a quick breath is the reaction I'm looking for. I carry her pink Coach bag to her home. We take our time getting to her house.

"Let me take you to dinner tomorrow?" I ask.

"I, well, if I go, I can't stay long. I'm still in college, and need to keep my grades up. A Lamil is always on the top of the dean's list, and I'm a Lamil." she says, seriously. The sun is high and I love it, but I see that she is squinting her eyes and picking up her pace, that sensitivity to heat and glare is a disadvantage of being human. This sun is perfect for my beast, it makes him feel at home.

"Okay, I can understand that. But I will ask something of you," I say. She stops and stares. I stare back. "Let's get you home before you cook," I say, moving faster and finally reaching her doorstep. I grab her again, tasting her lips, sucking and biting on them. She deepens the kiss, sliding her soft hands in my hair. Placing my hand on the back of her neck, I force her head back gently, giving me access to lick her long neck, pushing heat out of my tongue. The heat I release is very sensual, and better than any one of those rub creams humans use. She will be hot until I satisfy that craving. I turn, and whisper, "8:00 p.m.?"

"Yes."

I walk home quickly, not knowing if Cess can see, don't want to vanish if she's watching. I need to get to Hawken. If he thinks I'm going to let touching Cess slide, he is not the Hawk I know. As soon as I walk in my door, I yell.

"HAAAWKEN!" I stand still to wait for my brother. I'm sure Layern is on top of my feelings right now. I feel my nose flare, and as I'm taking a deep breath and exhaling, my breath is now a very deep purple smoke coming from my mouth and nose. I turn and see Hawken and Showken.

"Showken," I say, glaring at my brother Hawken.

"Listen, Draken, I didn't know you had already bedded her," Hawken says, glaring back. I move very fast, coming nose to nose with him. His beast is angry also, for I see his dark brown smoke coming out of his mouth. I don't want to fight, but I will.

"KEEP YOUR CLAWS OFF CESS!" I yell. I'm really trying not to burn him again. He says nothing, but turns, walking away. I calm my beast, watching my angry brother walking away. I will not stand for Hawken's tactics. He is known to make mistakes, but Cess will not be one of his mistakes, ever. Showken is just smirking at me.

"What?"

"I never thought The Great Draken would fall for anyone, but a human? This is awesome. Are you going to tell her what you are?" Showken asks.

"You're crazy, I don't love anybody, but if, and I mean if, I did, Cess could never know," I say.

"Why the hell not? Listen, if she is who you are going to marry, like Hawken says, she must know what she is getting into. What are you going to do if she sees you angry and breathing fire?"

"I'm not marrying that human, and she is not allowed to know. She would be killed in our land."

"When I want to marry, I marry whoever I want. Fuck tradition."

"Showken, you can't marry whoever you want. That is unheard of."

"Tell me this then, Draken, why do you still want a Giver

when you get married? Wait, I already know this answer. Because you don't even know if your chosen wife can satisfy your sexual needs, at least you know what a Giver brings. I'm marrying who I want, and if nobody likes it, oh well."

"Showken, I hope you're not disclosing that information to women you bed on earth. That is a serious crime. I could not get you out of this."

"Stop worrying."

"Showken."

"Draken. Come on brother, we did not eat enough at breakfast, lets go find food."

"Okay, but I really hope you're not telling anyone about us being dragons."

"I really hope you tell Cess, and then we all can get more relaxed, as she will be around a lot." Showken says. A smirk and laugh come from Showken.

"How do you know? She might not be around that much."

"It's in your eyes, and plus the gift you gave her in the hall. Don't worry, I shielded you both so the others could not see, but you've got it bad, brother, and she will be around a lot."

"I hate you, Showken," I say, smiling. We head to the kitchen and eat everything we can. As we laugh and crack jokes about Showken's absurd thinking, I can't help but think of Cess. Everyone thinks I love her when I don't. I want her body, but what if I'm wrong? I have never loved a woman before. I can't reveal my true self to Cess. She would run, and that is something I wouldn't want. I don't want her fear; I want her body. I must think on how to ensure the secret of my kind.

CESS

I'm such a slut! I can't believe I slept with Draken. Then, he actually went down on me in their very museum hall. They probably have cameras in the house. Oh God, I'm on camera, he has a sex tape of me. My father is going to kill me. Oh shit, he will kill Draken if it ever gets out. How could I be so stupid as to let him, wait, I'm jumping ahead. I'm thinking of the guys, I know Draken is a businessman, taping me would not benefit him. I'm going crazy. I need to just lie on my bed and think. I head to my room, and as I approach, who is there waiting? D.

"Hey, sis, have fun over at Kelly's house?" D asks, leaning on my door eating an apple. Using my twin sense, I narrow my eyes at D, damn it, he knows.

"Get away from my door," I say, pushing him off it.

"Well, are you going to tell me, or do I have to think of my own assumptions?"

"What do you want to know?" I ask, frowning.

"Hey, I'm just looking out for your best interests, but if my sis thinks she is over Travis, who, I might add, you wanted to marry, then I will accept your decision."

"I had a great time last night, that's all you need to know."

D pushes his way into my room, making his way to my lounge chair. Ugh, I don't want to talk about how slutty I was.

"Make yourself comfortable. I'm not talking, studying is what I'm doing," I say, walking inside my closet and closing the door. I put on a pair of shorts and a tank, hoping D will be gone when I come out.

"So, did you practice safe sex?"

"Yes," I lie.

"Are you seeing him again?"

"Yes."

"What is Dad going to say?"

"I'm not telling Dad, and neither are you."

"I would never rat you out," D says, "but Dad has a way of knowing things, and if it's Draken, you are not going to keep that hidden. I mean, you look like you fucked all night. I'm not judging, because you know how I do, but you fall in love very fast and hard. The next guy that breaks your heart is dealing with me."He rises up and heads for my door. "I love you, sis."

"I love you more," I say, understanding that my brother just wants the best for me. He leaves and shuts my door. I run to the mirror, and I do indeed look like I've been having sex all night. My lips are swollen, my face is still flushed and I'm hot as hell. I really feel like getting myself off. Why the hell I am I so horny? I need to go study. Forcing myself to sit, I keep moving my hips. Being with Draken was amazing. I can't believe how his brothers are so different, yet alike. That Hawken guy doesn't like me, but Showken is all smiles when he sees me. Showken is fun to be around. Then Gemi, you never know if he will talk or not, he is so handsome, though. Layern is unique, the way he answers my questions, and thoughts that are in my head, before I say them out loud. He must be psychic or something. Then there is Draken, damn, just thinking his name is making me hotter, it's like my lady garden is jumping. I really need some relief. Squirming in my chair, I slide my hand between my legs, holding myself and trying to make this urge go away. I need to stop this. What the hell is wrong with me? Draken more than satisfied me, in fact I don't think I did anything but scream his name. I should have been more active, that still does not explain my need for more. I mean, he even got me off in his hallway. I know, maybe a cold shower or something. I rush to my bathroom and turn on the shower. I get undressed fast and climb in. The coldness of the shower is taking away my need, but it only lasts a few seconds before I feel my body becoming more intense with the need to find release. I push my finger inside my sex, thinking of Draken. I find myself enjoying this, so I push two inside, fast. I need to come. Every time I get to the point of having some relief, it gets hotter. Getting out of the shower, I dry off, and walk naked to my bed. I can't study with this feeling. I have just climbed into bed, hoping for sleep, when my cell rings. Shit, it's Suzy.

"Hello?"

"Where were you? I've been calling your cell phone all night," Suzy says, "I wanted to tell you that Kelly hooked up with one of your neighbors last weekend at the party, and she says he rocked her world." I hear what she's saying, but I can't believe it. I rise from the bed, hoping it's not Draken.

"Who?" I snap. If Draken has had me and one of my good friends, I'm done.

"I think she said it was the one with blond hair. All I know is, she said it was the best she's ever had, but now he won't answer her calls and she is freaking out. Have you seen him with anybody new?"

"Oh, umm, no, I haven't seen anything."

"Well, umm, D called Kelly last night, asking about you. Then I got to thinking, that only happens when you're not at home, so spill. Who were you with last night, and why didn't I know?"

"Umm, D was looking for me? Well, I umm, stayed with Draken." I say, lowering my voice.

"What?"

"I spent the night with Draken." I repeat.

"AHHH, you and Kelly are getting some from those fine men. Oh, tell me everything, don't leave anything out!"

"Suzy!"

"Don't you Suzy me," she says, laughing. "This was the guy you said walked you off the property, now you're sleeping in his bed? I thought you said he was an ass? No, Cess, I want to know. Kelly seems not to remember what all her guy did, but I know you will tell your besty."

"Suzy, I didn't mean for it to happen. I was invited over for a party and-"

"Wait, it was a party and you didn't call me or anyone else? What kind of party was it?"

"The 'let's hook Cess and my brother up' kind of party. I was the only one invited. I know, before you say it, I'm a slut. Who sleeps with a man that she doesn't know? I'll probably get treated like Kelly, too."

"You will not get treated like Kelly, everyone knows she's a hoe. The blond haired one probably is not calling her back because she did some real freaky stuff. He knew what she was, but you, they had a party just for you? Get out! How is Draken? I bet he is awesome! Dang, you should have called me, that's why you weren't answering for me, you were busy!"

"I swear my phone never rang. Draken is amazing, he is so

gentle with me, which I needed since he is huge, like an anaconda. I mean, it hurt like hell at first, but then he was sweet and slow, pleased me beyond what I could imagine," I say.

"Wow, Cess, you sound really into this guy, and he was that good to make you go back on your promise. You stayed all night, too. When did you get home?"

"I just got in not too long ago. Oh, he ran me a bath and carried me to it. I was that sore, but he put a family tradition remedy or something in the water, and took all that away. I have a date with him tonight."

"Ahhh! I'm so happy for you. You are dating again, and with a big time CEO of a billion dollar company. Go Cess! So, do you think you will be spending another night?"

"God, I hope so."

"Oh, wow."

"It's just, ever since I came home, I've been extremely horny, and it's odd. Like, I need him or something to fill this need. I can't explain it, but my body is craving him," I say, frowning. I've never felt this way before. Travis and I had plenty of sex, and it never felt like this.

"Shit, Cess, that sounds so freaking hot. I love having sex with Luke, but never has my body ached or craved for him. Cess, what if he is like your soul mate or something? This is great."

"I'm not sure what it is, I just know that if I'm left alone with him tonight, I just don't want him to think I'm a slut, or easy."

"Cess, I'm sure he knows that. Besides, the only guy you truly have been with is Travis, Jeremy doesn't count, you were only 15 years old, and you never did it with him again," Suzy says, laughing.

"That's because Jeremy was such a prick. You're right, Travis is my only real sexual experience, but Suzy, I felt like a virgin with Draken. I mean, his hands were everywhere, I couldn't think at all. He is unreal in bed, I mean I don't have that much experience, but he didn't want to stop at all. He was even trying again this morning. Get this, the entire time I was sweating so bad, he never broke a sweat at all."

"I want sex like that."

"Well, I'm going to try to get some studying and school work done before my date tonight."

"Okay, but please tell me what happened when you get home, tonight or tomorrow." Suzy says, chuckling.

"Ha ha, goodbye, Suzy," I hang up the phone, slipping on a pair of shorts and a top, and go to the desk. I sit at the desk, turning on my laptop, and going straight to my paper on Juvenile Delinquency. I will work until it's time to get ready for Draken. I will go crazy if I think about last night. I get into school mode and start typing.

***

It's 7:00 p.m. before I know it. Saving my work, I push away from my desk and go to the shower. The heat is still there, and now that I'm done typing, it's getting really hot. Maybe it's because I'm going to see Draken. What am I going to wear? I mean, he's already seen me naked. He didn't say where dinner is going to be. I hope it's at a restaurant and not with his brothers, I like his brothers, except for a couple, but dinner out on a date sounds great. Besides, I may think more clearly when we are in public. Standing in front of my closet looking at dresses is exciting; I haven't been on a date in a long time. I'm trying to decide between showing my legs and showing my back, maybe both will work better than choosing one. Oh, this heat is getting unbearable. I know the air is on, but it won't hurt to check the gage in my room. I slide out my peach dress, smiling, knowing Draken is not going to be able to keep his eyes off me. I hope my dad and D don't scare him off. They can both be a little over-protective sometimes. I wonder why Draken has had this change of heart with me; I guess I should ask that question. Even though we have already been intimate, knowing this will help me process this thing we have. I mean, his brothers approached me before he did, which is really strange. Why would they do that? Draken is huge in the world of money and business, which goes hand in hand with the way I've been raised. He's single, handsome, well-built, is an unreal lover, and has an animal side to him as well. I haven't seen this side, yet I know it's there. His low growls when he kissed me were so sexy, I want to hear those growls again. Just thinking of it makes me hot all over again. This man has me in a trance, and I need to figure him out. He wants six months, I'll give him a month and see how we are together. It might work, I've always been really mature, and I don't know his age, I'm guessing around twenty-six or twenty-seven years old. Although he has this wise look on his face, he may be very mature like me, too. Oh, I got a date tonight!

After I finally sit down at my vanity to do my makeup, I hear the doorbell ring. Draken, I hope you can deal with my father, he's all alpha, and the interrogations about me will begin soon. I take my time doing my eyes, pulling my hair up in a soft bun, making sure some hair is falling out of the bun in the front and back. I hear the door. Then my mother walks in.

"Oh, Princess, you look fabulous. I just met the young man taking you out. He is very handsome and a charmer. I did want to know, did you know he is 29 years old? Before you get upset, I think he is perfect, but guys his age, baby, are looking to settle down, start a family. I just want you to know what you are dealing with," my mother says.

"I did not ask his age, mother, but 29 years old is fine with me. I'm not going to be settling down and having babies any time soon. Thanks for being such a good mom. It's just a date, no harm in having fun, right? Besides, I'm sure dad is down there telling him what he wants for me, and how he is not it," I say, remembering when he met Travis.

"Actually, dear, he is having a drink with him and laughing. In fact, I believe your father sees this as a chance to expand the Lamil family wealth. Do you even know how much his family is worth?" she asks, with a beautiful smile.

"No, Mom, and I really don't care. We already have money, so him having money is just a plus."

"Princess, yes, we have money, but it's been rumored the Draglen brothers, specifically Draken, are like a treasure cave, the amount is endless. He owns a few islands, darling, so if you did want a long-lasting relationship with him, you have my blessing. Princess, you deserve nothing less than a man like Draken."

"Well, it's just a date, okay, let me go to dinner."

"Okay, that sounds good. One other thing, you're still using your pills, right?"

"Yes, Mom, please don't make me more embarrassed."

"Princess, that is a man downstairs, not a boy, he will want sex, and no babies unless you have his name."

"Can I finish my last touches on my face in private?"

"Of course, I'll let him know you're coming right down."

"Thanks."

***

We have a very quiet table for two at Elements. It's a very upscale restaurant. I've been here numerous times, but love to go whenever

I can. There is silence between us. I really don't know what to say. My body has been blazing since he touched my hand, when I walked in to see him and my father laughing and shaking hands. My father even told me to have a good time, and winked at me. Draken has made an impression on my father and mother, but D's opinion is what I really want. My brother and I are twins, and we have a strong bond. Draken pulls me from my thoughts.

"So, Princess, I find it strange you don't go by your name," he says, sipping wine. My father and mother just had to speak about me using my unusual name.

"I, uh, really don't like it. My parents forgot that I wouldn't stay a baby when they named me, so I go by Cess," I say, feeling uncomfortable. Why did they have to say my name, they could have just said "my daughter".

"Well, I like Princess, and I will call you by your birth name, not a made-up one. I think it says something that they would give you a name of high esteem. You should be proud of your name, Princess," he says, smiling at me. I'm squirming in my seat looking into those purple eyes. I mean my God, he is so handsome, sexy and has me hot from his stare. But I will not consent to being called Princess. I must correct this.

"Draken," I say, "Though I appreciate your opinion on how I should be proud of my name, I would prefer you to call me Cess. That is the name I told you, and it's my name, and if I want to use my nickname then you should respect my wishes and call me Cess.

Not some ridiculous name my parents have given me." I find my voice is higher in tone when I get to the last sentence. He is staring at me, rubbing his chin. I love a perfectly trimmed goatee. He is rubbing his chin slowly and staring at me. No smile, just a stare. I hope he's not mad. Then he abruptly breaks the stare, and the waiter is at our table.

"May I order for you, Princess," he says, and I notice his eyes are now a darker purple. Shit, he must be pissed.

"Yes, please, Draken. And it's Cess." I'm going to stand my ground. I will not be bullied, I'm a Lamil, and I value what Grandfather says, "Always stand your ground." I stare back at him, and he gives me a smile that says I'm in trouble. Shit. He looks at the guy taking the order.

"To start," Draken says, "we both will have steamed clams, tomato and beer soup, the watercress salad. For dinner, umm, the pan roasted duck looks good. We won't need dessert. That will be all." He hands the waiter our menu. Why no dessert, I like dessert. His eyes are piercing my soul. I can't break the stare. My body is heating up and I just want to be under him right now. I can't believe he still called me Princess after I asked him not to, now no dessert. I look at him and he's smirking at me. The menace is smirking at me.

"Not cool, at all," I snap. "I may have wanted dessert." I raise a brow at him.

"Princess, not in public."

"Not in public, what?"

"Hmm, I want you too, Princess."

"Stop calling me that, Draken!" I say, through my teeth.

"We're going to have so much fun tonight. I know our first time was unexpected, but tonight, Princess, you will know what is coming. You look so beautiful, those brown eyes will be my downfall, yet I can't wait for dessert, until then, let's get to know each other over dinner." He speaks just above a whisper and his pissed, commanding voice is enough for me to table this argument.

"Fine, why don't you tell me about yourself?"

"Nah, you first, Princess. What kind of man do you think I am?" he says, as our first course arrives. I take this moment to dig in. I think you are a man who is making me go back on my promise.

"Umm, there's not much to tell. I turn 21 in about a couple of months."

"What day?"

"Umm, July 27th. Don't interrupt," I say, smiling. "I'm a senior in college and graduating soon. This is my last term, and I'm counting the days. I plan on moving out, starting my life. That's pretty much it."

"Really? Tell me about dancing," he asks.

"Dancing? Well, I love to dance. I have always wanted to be a dancer, but if you're a Lamil, you either go into the family business or something the family approves of. Dancing is not on the list of approvals," I say, getting a little teary-eyed. I can't share my emotions with this guy. Cess, pull it together, way too deep for a first date.

"Don't."

"Don't what?"

"Don't ever be ashamed to tell me your feelings, they are always important," Draken says, getting my attention. The heat between us is flaming. This is going to be a long dinner.

DRAKEN

Her name is very fitting. She has some nerve giving me orders. I have never had a Giver like this. Princess, yes, I like it. In fact, I will make it a point to say her name often, reminding her. Dancing is her passion, and when she talks about it there's a spark, but when she mentions her life after college, I only feel sadness. Princess is very special. Dinner is going to get hot.

"Draken, tell me about you. I think I've shared more information than you."

"Oh, everything I would share, you can Google," I say, looking into those eyes. There is something about them.

"Ah, come on, that's not fair. If you don't say anything, I'm done talking."

"That's fine," I say. I love food. Human food is just like ours, sort of, we just have some different ways of cooking. The silence is going to kill me out in public, all I can hear is everyone's heartbeat, feel their heat and sense their wants. I need her to talk.

"Okay, fine, I'll talk. I come from a large family. We are very close, and nice," I say, stopping my thoughts.

"And-" Damn, I just want to take those sexy legs and grab them right here, on this table, and make her scream. That sexy mouth is very tempting. I will wait until later.

"And, there is nothing else about me, what is your favorite color?" I need these questions to fall in her direction, I want to know more about her, she doesn't need that much information on me.

"What? It's, umm, purple."

"Really?"

"Yes, and yours?" She is becoming more tempting by the minute.

"Purple, do you want to know why?" What the hell am I doing?

"Yes, please." Oh, I want this girl bad. You will say please, Princess.

"It's my color, it gives me strength, it shows who I am most of all, which is very important in my family and my land."

"Where are you from, you don't have an accent. You always say "my land". What country are you from?"

"This is your land, and I'm from a different place, and in my land, I do have an accent and different language." She bites on her bottom lip again. I can't wait until she's my Giver, she will be singing a new language.

"So, you have secrets, Draken Draglen." She smiles, and it deserves an award. Yes, she could break a heart.

"Using my full name I see, well, some things I just can't tell you, without your life being compromised," I say. I'm waiting for the fear to set in, but nothing comes, just more curiosity. Fuck!

"If you know my father, which I know you do, I don't scare easily, I usually scare other people."

"Princess, hurry and eat. I'm done, and would like my dessert," I say. She's very interesting.

"What is my dessert?"

"Me. I think you're done. Come, let's go take a late swim in the pool." I rise, hoping she does as she told without any questions. I notice the twist in her hips, she's stirring in the chair, ahhh, my heat is all over her. I'll have to take care of her soon. She stands, and that dress does wonders for her body, and those legs are going to be my downfall.

"Okay, since you asked so nicely."

"I told you, I'm nice," I laugh, for the first time in a while, it's natural. I like that feeling.

"You should laugh more often," she says, reaching for her purse.

"Why?"

"It's the first time you've seemed real and relaxed, and… I think it's sexy." The heat is growing very fast, the pool might be later if she keeps this up. I've never had someone compliment me without wanting something, in my homeland or this land.

"Come on, Princess, I have plans for you tonight," I say, linking arms with her as we head out. She whispers, "You know we didn't pay the bill, right?"

"Yes I did," I chuckle.

"When?" She stops, looking confused and sexy as hell. I guess I'll tell her.

"When I bought it, three years ago," I say, walking out. My car is waiting, and we get in.

"You own it? You could have just told me, Draken, it's no big deal. You know I don't want anything from you, I have my own inheritance," she snarls. I like her courage.

"Princess, please save your energy, you'll need it."

"So, you're really not going to call me Cess?"

"No, your name is Princess, and that is what I shall address you as, my zell."

"What is zell?" Why did I just call her that, fuck, I'm not supposed to speak Magen in front of humans.

"Nothing bad, turn the radio on, I like music."

"Okay," she says, smiling. It's a smooth ride to my house.

***

"Get in the water, Princess." How can she be shy about getting nude into the water? I have her entire body in my head already.

"Your brothers are here, besides, they were already giving me a look."

"Who gave you a look?" My voice drops, until it's almost a whisper.

"Draken, they all are looking at me like I'm a slut." Princess says, pouting. "I just know it, and we never have discussed why 6 months, why me? I'm scared to get naked in the pool with your brothers here," I see she needs incentive. I climb out of the water, totally nude. Walking really slowly, I want her to see me. I'm not ashamed of my body. I get extremely close, taking her purse and setting it on the outdoor table. I grab her wrist and start licking her entire hand as if it were ice cream. When her eyes widen, I take her by surprise and give her a hard, forceful kiss. She moans, just as I'm placing my tongue deep in her mouth. I get that dress off quickly, and now I see she didn't have on a bra.

"Look at you, so beautiful," I say, holding her away slightly.

"Draken, you snake. You got me naked, anyway."

"Snake, no my dear, beast is a better name for me," I say, pitching her into the water in her thong and heels. I'll buy her another pair of heels.

"DRAAAKEN!" she screams, but she is in, and I dive right in

after her. She comes up looking beautiful, hair slicked back and no longer pulled up. I grab her from behind.

"Yes, Princess?"

"You are so sneaky, I'm in this water naked now," she laughs, and I know she is as excited as I am to have sex with her in this pool. She is still wearing clothing, though. I dive under the water and snatch off that thong. "Ahhhh, I'm going to kill you, Draken!"

"Yes you are," I say, before I can think. Princess is very dangerous to me. I want to tell her everything. I love to see her laugh, and she makes me feel great. Yes, she will be my downfall.

"What kind of statement is that, Draken? You know I'm not a killer. It's just a figure of speech, you know. Well, maybe not in your land, but in mine, it's said sometimes for fun, not for real."

"Come, let me have a kiss," I say, moving in close. I circle her, feeling her anticipation.

"Yes, you can have a kiss."

"Back up against the wall," I say, controlling my beast. He wants out.

"Why do your eyes turn dark purple sometimes?" she asks, panting. Yes, she is feeling the heat. I don't answer her. I push her up against the wall of the pool, dive under and begin to kiss the lips between those sexy legs. She never expected this. She tugs at my hair, causing me to give her a little bite. I'll stop when I'm ready. I hear her begging.

"Yes, ohh yes, it feels so, ohh . . . please, your brothers . . .

ohhh, ahhhhhh!" I finally come up, once I've had my fill. She is panting something unbelievable. The look on her face is priceless, and I want to see more of it.

"Stay the night?"

"Draken, you take my breath away. You have me naked in your pool while your brothers are so close, and then you just, ohh you just…"

I kiss her gently.

"Please," I ask, and my heat expands outward. I can't pull it back. Fuck!

"Draken, this water is getting really warm, what kind of pool is this?" Princess says, looking at the water. Please, water don't boil. I don't have time to explain.

"Let's get out of the water and go to my room, okay?"

"Okay," I help her out of the water, keeping her face forward as I walk her to a door that leads to my room.

"Draken, my clothes,"

"Don't worry, Princess, I'm going back to get them now. You just stay here and I will be right back," I say, licking her lips. I slip on a pair of pants, and quickly go back to the pool. I notice Layern and Showken are standing there, arms crossed. I see our pool now looks like a freaking hot spring. Fuck!

"Yeah, fuck is the right thought," Layern says, frowning. I'm losing control, why did Princess have to come down the street?

"Draken, this is going way too far," Showken says, arms

folded across his chest. "I'm with you no matter what, brother, but if you are going to be with her, risking our secret, you need to make a decision. Brother, you are, well I have never seen you like this with anyone, not even Ravla, and she has been around for over a hundred years." He looks serious.

"I know it looks bad when our pool has heated to a very high degree, but I have it under control," I say, picking up Princess' clothes in record time. "Wait, what are you asking?" I growl. They can't be asking me to give her up.

"You pulling her into our world," Layern says, narrowing his eyes. "And I felt her noticing the pool getting warm, Draken. You need to decide if she is going to be a true Giver, as you say, then tell her, claim her, and be done with this." I'm nose to nose with him in no time.

"You, know I can't claim her as a true Giver, she's human and has a life here. That would result in her leaving her land. You let me handle this and you cool the pool. NOW!" I growl. I see Showken moving closer.

"Do you think, could you feel," Showken says, titling his head like a predator. "What I'm trying to say is I've been reading the Aumdo. I found that if a Dragon who is heir to the throne has not taken a wella or wife, he may choose her. Do you see what I'm getting at?"

Covering my eyes with my hand, I try to get a handle on what Showken has read. I hold out my hand for the book and it immediately appears. Another perk of being a Dragon: if I want it, I will have it. Opening the section on having a wella, I read past all the tradition and come to the part to which Showken is referring. I glance up, noticing my brothers' looks of confusion. Layern instantly pushes on my thoughts. What is it about her that makes me want her so badly? I continue reading, going farther into the Aumdo. The Aumdo is like our rule-book, it has been around forever. If it's in the rule-book, it can be done.

"I'm going back to my Giver, she is waiting for me," I say, rising and sending the book back to its place. Grabbing Princess' clothes, I head back to my room. I will not discuss this now. I come in to find her sleeping under the sheets, tossing and turning, looking very beautiful. She is hot, I must fill her need. I climb in, wrapping my arm around her waist. I pull her very close and begin kissing her back, my heat for her begins to rise. Hmm, she tastes so good.

"Princess, turn and lie on your back, I will ease the burning," I whisper in her ear. She turns towards me and starts kissing me, pulling at my hair, holding me tightly and moaning. Between every kiss she says, "Mmm, yes, I need you," I realize it's been too long. I slide on top of her, holding myself up to see her body. It's more than I can handle, my control is being lost; I need to be inside her. I take her legs with both hands, holding them in the air, and see her sex all hot and wet for me. I make eye contact, and we stare for a second, then I dip down and suck her clitoris, giving her an instant

138

climax.

"DRAAAAKEN!" she yells. I continue to suck her folds, dipping my tongue in and out of her, making sure to get every drop of her sweet cream, it's mine. "Oh, please," she begs, panting.

"Princess, I will take care of you, just enjoy," I whisper, looking up at her face. She is red. "Scream if you want, cry, scratch, bite, it will not bother me. You feel free, my Princess," I say, and I realize I said "my Princess", do I feel that way? I look at her again, and she is so wet for me, crying out my name with such need. I've never had a Giver like this. Lifting up those beautiful legs onto my shoulders, I let my hands slide down her legs as I enter her. She weakens me, and I find I need to close my eyes to gain composure. Throwing my head back in pleasure, I feel the beast scales coming in on my chest. Fuck! I can't even stop my stirring of her sex, I just hope she doesn't notice.

"Please don't stop."

I see her eyes are closed. I feel relief to let my beast out some with her. What is happening to me? I knew she would be my downfall.

I rise, pulling her with me. Kneeling, I hold her in place as I continue to give her the pleasure she needs. I feel everything about her. The connection is becoming very intense, and she begins to ride me, twisting her body in very satisfying ways. "More, I need you," she moans. I need her, too. Grabbing her hair, I pull her head back, exposing her neck, and as she rides I send her heat. I begin licking and sucking her neck as her head is pulled back. Her body is shivering, yet I want more. I can't get deep enough. "Ahhh, fuck!" I yell. My back is turning dark purple, I know. Princess is going to meet my beast. I begin to send images of our love-making in a forest, at the same time sending quick shots of me in Dragon form. I need her to see. I may want her as a Giver, forever.

"Drake . . . ohh . . . yes . . . umm . . . I see . . . ohh, YESSS!" she screams. I smile, knowing she is enjoying me.

"Yes, Princess, give it to me, release it all," I whisper into her chest, taking in a breast and sucking hard.

"Climax, Princess," I say, watching her body react to my words. It gives me great pleasure to watch her, she is fascinating, for a human. I've never met one that could get me to want her, never. I can't see anyone but her.

"Draken, I, I, oh-," Princess tries to speak, but she soon finds her release. Sleep takes over right away again, and now I have a very limp Princess who is asleep or blacked out. I ease out of her, laying her down in the bed. She is so red. I haven't released, because I need to figure out what Princess is to me. I climb out of bed, and stand thinking. Could Princess be more than a Giver? What will she remember of the visions I gave her during sex? Will she accept me enough to be a Giver, or something else? I head to my bathroom and shut the door. Placing my hands on the counter, I look into the mirror and see my beast staring back at me.

"Yes, I know she is amazing, but you might scare her."

"I am you," my beast says to me. We can communicate with each other, one cannot function without the other. "Make her understand."

"No, I will have her as a Giver and that's it. Wella would be too much for her, me and my people."

"My people, too, and I say we have her," my beast growls, standing up in the mirror, showing he is standing his ground.

"We will see," I say, sitting on the floor. Ravla is calling, shit, I forgot as a Giver she would need her Taker sometimes. Ignoring the plea she is sending me in my head, I get up and join Princess in bed. Watching her sleep, I show her some quick clips of us. I will enter her dream and show her more. I need to find out what her reaction is to all this. My brothers want her to know, but I know if she resists, she could be put to death or taken to my land. We can never allow her to know and start to tell people. They might think she was crazy, but clearly it would be a mess. Let me see what her mind thinks. I close my eyes, relaxing, going into Princess' dream.

CESS

Why am I in a forest? There are birds flying, and little night things flying away. Oh, I'm dreaming. Draken gave me an orgasm that made me black out. I need this too, he didn't get his yet, that is really odd because I heard him yell out, but he kept going. He is such a great lover. I guess I will sleep in this dream. Just thinking about Draken is making me want him. That is when it really hits me.

"I'm in a forest, lying in his bed still. This is not going to be good," I say out loud. I really start to look around, and the trees are huge, like hundred-foot trees, and they are so pretty with different colored leaves. I glance up, hearing a noise, and I see a man standing in the distance. It's dark, I can't see his face. Then, he steps into the light, shit I'm dreaming of Draken, again.

"Draken, you're in my dreams. Why are you standing so far away, come close and see me," I yell. I mean it's a dream, I can be as bad as I want, maybe even tell him I may be falling for him, and it's only been a couple of times of hot sex and dinner. He begins to walk toward me in nothing but black pants, no shoes, no shirt. His hair is down, and he looks beautiful as he comes closer. God, he's so handsome. I notice as he walks closer that his eyes are bright, and deep purple. He still doesn't speak.

"Draken, why are you not speaking, it's my dream, you have to do what I say." He smiles.

"Yes, Princess."

"Draken, my dream, my rules. It's Cess."

"Even in your dream, Princess."

"Draken I-" I hear a noise and loud footsteps, coming close. What is that? This should be a good dream, but it is not. I turn to tell Draken, and he is right there beside me, looking in the direction the noise is coming from.

"Draken, do you hear that?"

"Yes, I do, Princess, don't be scared."

"What, I don't like this dream, this is turning into a freaking nightmare." I pull the covers close, noticing I'm still naked. Ohhh shit, how is this dream so real?

"Wake up Cess, wake up," I begin to repeat.

"Princess, take a breath, I'm here, nothing is scarier than me. I will protect you. What do you think it is?" Turning, I notice the trees are shifting, literally moving, making a path for whatever it is. Okay, this is a dream. I should not be scared.

"Draken, umm . . . I've got to pee. I usually have to pee when I get frightened. And I'm naked in this dream. Why couldn't I have dreamed I had on clothes, so I could run? I know, I'm rambling right now, but have you ever heard if you die in your dream you die in real life? And right now, I think we are about to die in a dream." I hear a very loud roar. I jump on Draken.

"Princess, it will be fine, you're frightening him."

"What, you know what it is, Draken, I'm never dreaming about you again, we should be having sex not waiting for . . . OHHH SHIT! AHHHHHHH!" This dream is so weird. The dinosaur just sits down and watches me.

"Draken, there is a dinosaur in my dream! There's a dinosaur watching me!"

"Princess, it's me, and not a dinosaur, either."

"Draken, you must be scared or crazy, you are right here with me in the bed that . . . how big is it, fifty feet tall?"

"No, about sixty-eight feet."

"Draken, this is no time for jokes, I'm really scared, what if it's hungry?"

"You're in a dream, remember, you are in control, just think like that, okay?" I stare at it and its eyes are so . . . shit! I turn very slowly, Draken's eyes are the same as this beast's eyes.

"Draken, what did you mean, it's you?" He smiles, and I hear a rumble from it, like it wants my attention. I study this beast more. It's purple, with light and dark shades mixed in together. I notice its wings. It's actually a very beautiful creature.

"It won't harm you, Princess. Would you like to come closer?"

"Are you crazy, we will just sit in bed until I wake up."

"Come, lets get closer, we don't have much time."

"I'm naked, Draken, why can't we lie in bed and have more hot sex, I promise to be more active."

He tilts his head in confusion. "Princess, you are very active. Now, come." He stands, holding out his hand. I'm not moving. If it's my dream, I can do what I want, and I want to sit here and watch this.

"If it's not a dinosaur, what is it?"

"A dragon."

"Shit, we really are dead. I'm dreaming of purple dragons. This should be a really hot dream."

"It will be, Princess. I see I must take some control." He whips the sheet off me. "You are so beautiful; now stand up, so I can wrap the sheet around you."

"You are so demanding," I say, grabbing his hand. He is pulling me from my comfort zone, and the need to pee comes back.

"Draken, I have got to pee, I'm scared." He places a hand on my abdomen, and the urge is gone.

"How did you do that?"

"One day I might tell you, now, let me introduce you."

"What! You know dragons?" I ask, and I know my eyes are like a deer's in headlights. I begin to walk and the ground is soft, really soft. I look down and it's purple, like walking on feathers.

"I know this one very well." We stop twenty feet away from it. I watch its eyes and they blink. I go to jump back, and Draken is behind me like a wall. He grabs my hand, and though I struggle, I end up right in front of its mouth, and it's huge, like, movie huge. Its mouth is closed, and makes a sound like a sigh once I'm there.

"Stroke him, he wants you to rub his head." Draken is serious. It's a dream, right? I reach out and rub the snout. It's soft, and a huge sigh comes from it, and out of the nostrils comes a light purple smoke. It's unreal. I continue to rub the dragon's snout.

"Draken, what's going on?"

"I wanted you to meet all of me."

"Are you saying you can get really mean?" I ask, taking another step, moving towards the dragon's neck, noticing a necklace filled with huge jewels.

"I'm saying this is me, too, and you have all of me now. My beast likes you, Princess."

"Draken, you're talking crazy, you're not a dragon," I say, smiling at him. He looks a little pissed when I say that. Damn.

"What if I were, Princess? Would you still be with me, can I still lick your juices as you climax?"

146

"Umm . . . yes I would, if this was a part of you, I would still want you, Draken," I say, looking right at his face. He relaxes and gives me a huge smile. I've never seen him smile like that.

"Come, let's get into bed so you get your wet dream," he says, leading me from the dragon, who I can swear is whimpering.

"Oh, yes, sounds good to me." We end up back in the bed in the forest, and we are both naked. I didn't see him take his pants off, but he is hovering over me, speaking another language. We are kissing very passionately when I notice the dragon is watching closely.

"Draken, it's watching."

"I know, your body is beautiful to look at," he says, bending to kiss my neck. He seems like he is happy about something. I wonder.

"Draken, I'm not scared any more, you're right, it didn't harm me, but it still looks like it could if it wanted to."

"It will never, now shhh, I'm enjoying you." I feel him lingering between my folds, and I push against him in need, and he fills me up. This dream is getting better. This feels so good, and a little weird having the dragon watch, but Draken feels so good inside me. It's like I'm his and he is mine.

***

"Ohhh . . . Yes . . . It feels so gooood!" I scream out. Opening my eyes, I'm awake in bed with Draken. It was a dream, a very weird dream though. I can't even think straight when he keeps licking my lady garden, then thrusting inside me with his penis, it's heavenly torture.

"Princess, grab your legs by your ankles and lift them in the air. I want you to hold them, no matter what, okay?"

"Uhh, okay," I pull my legs up by the ankles, but I'm so sweaty my hands are slipping. I try to hold them up. He is doing long licks, holding my folds apart. There is no way I can hold them up.

"Hold them up, Princess, I feel you trembling."

"Draken, please."

"Please, what?"

"I don't know, just please."

"Okay, Princess, let me, I'll hold them up."

"Ohhh, okay." Oh, he is taking turns from licking my sex, to thrusting inside me. He is thrusting in . . . out . . . in . . . out. I'm losing it, this is too much. Ohhh, he's back to licking me again, oh shit, he has lifted me into the air, my ass is off the bed. I think I love him. Oh, he is licking me from my butt up until he reaches my clitoris.

"Draken, I can't take it. You . . . ohhh . . . wait . . . YESSSSS!" he is thrusting again in . . . out . . . in . . . out.

"Princess, climax for me and I'll join you." That is what I need, and I feel like a waterfall has hit me. I'm climaxing and so is he. Oh my, he looks amazing. He does not slouch on me afterwards. He lies next to me, panting now. I turn my head and face him, and he is smiling.

"Draken, that . . . you . . . trying to make me fall in love?" I smile.

"Would that be bad?" He raises an eyebrow. What? He can't be serious.

"You are amazing, Draken, you're spoiling me. You know when this is over, I may not want another man unless he is like you," I say, not thinking.

"You are mine, Princess, if another tries to touch you I may lose my cool."

"I like you, Draken, more than I should, this is way too comfortable," I say, ducking my head into his chest. It's extremely hot. I mean, the heat is radiating off him. Is he sick? "You're really hot, you think you're getting sick?"

"First, I never get sick, and second, I always get very hot when I'm happy. Now, would you like a bath?"

"Draken, I have to go home," I look at his clock on the table. Damn, it's after midnight already. "Draken, my dad is not going to like me staying the night with you. I have to go home. I'm sorry."

"You have to let me bathe you, then you go home, not before, okay?" he says. He has the most captivating light purple eyes I've ever seen.

"I'm going to have to learn to say no to you. Okay, but a very quick bath, Draken, I don't want my parents to know what we've been doing." I kiss his chin, moving up his body to find his lips. Shit, I'm sore.

"I'll start the water, don't move," he says, walking to the bathroom.

"I can't, don't worry. I have to get my legs cooperating," I laugh. My dream starts coming back to me. In my dream, Draken says, the dragon is him. Why would he say that? He comes back, standing next to the bed.

"You ready for a bath?"

"Yes, Draken . . . you are such a gentleman." I go to slide out of bed, and he has me in his arms, carrying me.

"Well, thank you, Princess. I had better make sure you are always carried to bathe."

He leans in, kissing me gently. Draken is stealing my heart, and I'm not sure it will be safe with him. I smile, and let him carry me to my bath. I still can't shake that dream.

DRAKEN

Princess is pulling at me. She stroked my beast, and I love her touch. I want more of it. Carrying her to the bath seems only right, when I have made sure she can't walk after sex. I really enjoy her body. She gets dressed, and I walk her home. She's coming in after 2:00 am, but she's coming home. That is not what I want. I give her an approval kiss, sensing her brother near at the door, and walk back to my car. If my Princess thinks the night is over, she is wrong.

***

I walk to the fridge for food. Princess is draining. I'm eating all sorts of food, steak, chicken, chips, cookies, soda, fruit and veggies, anything I can get my hands on. When Hawken comes in, I don't have time for him.

"What?" I say, not looking up from the counter.

"Brother, why are you so cold with me?"

"Not tonight, Hawken, another day," I say.

"Tonight, right now."

"Hawken, I'm warning you, leave me alone," I growl.

"I don't hate you."

"I know, Hawken, I'm hungry, I need to eat, long night ahead," I say, remembering my plans for Princess.

"About that." I raise my head and glare at him. For his sake, I hope he doesn't piss me off. It's too late to be burning brothers who are dragons. "Listen, you have a bride being prepared for you, and you have fallen for a human, I don't mind, it's you, I just wonder how our land will accept her, if you bring a human into our land to be with you on the throne. I don't think that will fly. A war could break out, brother, just think of us all. That is all I will say about her."

"I know," I say, "there is a bride waiting for me back home. Right now, I have a Giver, she may not know she is a Giver, but she is. I will worry about things later. I will protect the land, our family and the throne, so, brother, thank you for your concern. I will always make the right decision."

152

"Thanks brother, and if you do choose to be with her, I will fight for you. I may fight you, but I'm your brother. If any other, then they deal with me."

"Dorli Hawken."

"Dorli Draken." This is our way of apologizing. I finish the last of the food, wash my hands and make my way to Princess' room using my powers.

I must use my powers to get into her bed. Closing my eyes, I appear in her bedroom. Princess looks so peaceful, but I want more of her. I climb into her Victorian-style bed. Wrapping my arms around her, I plant soft kisses on her face until she opens her eyes.

"Mmmm, is this a dream?" she says, turning her body into me. She is only wearing a t-shirt.

"No," I say. "I'm really here in your room. If you won't stay the night with me, well here I am." I kiss her neck.

"Draken, this house is huge and our rooms are not that close, but I tend to scream with you and . . . it's my parents' house."

"Ahh, you are worried in case someone hears you begging for more, or screaming my name," I say, parting her legs and placing my hand in between her thighs, cupping her sex.

"Both, to be honest. How did you get in? Security is on. My brother D was waiting up for me, asking twenty questions about you," Princess says, moving her body with my hand. Yes, Princess, enjoy my touch.

"I'll talk with your brother, he should be worried about you.

What brother wouldn't be worried about his twin? Besides, I need to get to know those you love," I say, feeling her come close. She is panting now, leaning in she starts the kiss, owning my mouth. I love her aggression.

"Princess, let me get you out of this shirt, no clothes from now on. I may stop in at night, and clothes should not cover this body when we are alone, okay?" I say, pulling the shirt over her head. I can't resist, her nipples are hard and ready. I take them in my mouth and she cries out, asking for more. I shield her room, not wanting interruptions.

"Draken, please,"

"Please what?"

"You know, I need you," I continue my assault on her firm breasts, licking and biting softly, making her beg for more. I want her so used to my touch that she does, without me asking.

"Okay Princess, lie on your back and lift your legs. I want them on my shoulders." She does it without hesitation. Her beautiful legs in the air, waiting for me, are a wonderful sight. I climb out, get undressed and get back in. I wrap her legs around my waist, leaning in, and when her tongue meets mine, I begin softly kissing her mouth. I take the kiss deep, giving her a small amount of heat. I will be slow tonight, I want to see and feel her body, my body. She is mine. Princess has me so confused about my feelings for her. I should not be sneaking into her room, yet here I am, craving her body. The thought that this will end in six months saddens me. I've never been in love and I'm 427, sooner or later a dragon stops hoping. I have known since I could fly that a bride was going to be prepared for me. I thought I could defer that and fall in love. It never happened, but here I am with Princess. She awakens feelings in me that should not be. I can never fall for a human, and never plan on it. I will get these emotions under control and place her in a proper role, as a Giver. Right now, I will continue to enjoy her soft moans for me. Princess will be my Giver, nothing more.

CESS

THREE MONTHS LATER

It's the day before my last final. I can't believe I'm truly getting ready to be done with college. I've worked really hard and now I'm going to be done with school. Draken and I have been dating now for 2 ½ months. I had to make him say the word officially "dating". He did not want to say it, but I put my foot down and let him know I was not doing the "friends with benefits" thing. If he wants to have sex, then I need a title. I'm getting ready to go meet some of my classmates on campus. I need to study away from the house, or else Draken will come by, or I'll be at his house, and studying will not get done. I'm so happy D and Draken have found something in common, hiking. D loves the outdoors and so does Draken. I grab my purse and go to the door, where the Maserati is waiting for me. I jump in with a grin, and start driving to go study. When my cell phone starts ringing, I roll my eyes. I should have known. The joy of living so close to Draken.

"Yes?"

"Where are you going?" Draken says, in that voice that I've come to adore.

"Uhh, remember, last final tomorrow. I'm going to study," I say, smiling.

"Why? You can study here. I promise to let you get your studying done, then we can have a celebration."

"No, you know that will not work. Besides, stop with that voice you're giving me, you know what that does to me. I'll be back in a few hours and-"

"A few hours, Princess, that's too long, I . . . You should have said it would be that long. I would have gone with you," he says. Draken is extremely jealous. He doesn't want anybody touching me, and wants to know my whereabouts all the time. I thought it would pass, but the more time I spend with him, the more possessive he becomes. I should be scared, but I'm not, I think I love him. I won't tell him that, since he already told me six months in the beginning. I won't think about that, it makes me cry that he will leave soon, time has flown by.

"Draken, don't make this a big deal. I will be back soon,

besides, I want to see you, too."

"Okay, Princess, I have some business I need to take care of, so I will be waiting for you when you pull up. Yes, if you drive by my house and don't stop, I'll ask something of you, Princess."

"Really? I like when you ask something from me. I'm always benefiting," I say, laughing loudly.

"Hurry back, and remember, I don't like guys touching you. Please, don't let anything happen that will upset me."

"Draken, no, I'm not going there with you. I'll talk with you later." I hang up. I'm sure I just pissed him off. Oh well, this 'no one can touch you without my permission' sounds crazy. I pull up to the school and park, stopping in the café to get an iced mocha. I find my study buddies in Carney Hall.

"Hello everyone," I say, assessing who is in the room. There are only five of us. The others are such slackers, Kyle, Rachel, Scott, and Linda are good students. Kyle is a sweetheart and is going to make some woman happy one day. Right now, he is all about his career and excelling. Rachel is a brat, but she is very smart, and has never received lower than a B in school her entire life. She still hates Mr. Garland, her 9th grade gym teacher. Linda is very much a nerd. She is not up-to-date on anything but education, which is fine, I just hope one day she sees how pretty she is. Linda could have any man she wants, she's that beautiful, that is why I keep her away from Draken, he could see past the crazy clothes. Then there is Scott, he is such a pretty boy in all ways. He is very popular and has always wanted to date me, but I've never seen us being together. What most people don't know is that Scott is not just a pretty face, he is actually very smart, and will be able to do anything he chooses in life, not to mention he's a Nolan, and they are known for many things, including their wealth.

"Hey, Cess, I didn't think you were going to make it," Rachel says.

"I'm here, so what are we going over first? Theories, I'm sure the final will be some sort of essay," I say, sitting around the table with the others. I pull out my books and papers, as Scott starts his compliments.

"Cess, you sure smell good, as usual," Scott says, with a huge smile on his face. He is such a flirt, if Draken was here he would go crazy.

"Thank you, Scott, for noticing how I smell, but I'm here to study."

"Me, too. So, Cess, can I see your thoughts on capital punishment?" Kyle asks. I hand him my notes, while Linda and Rachel exchange theirs. "I think we will be tested on everything we have learned in Mrs. Garcia's class this term. We have four hours tomorrow for the final, so I've been preparing for-" Scott brushes my hair out of my face as I lean down, and a sharp pain hits me out of nowhere. I can't think about that right now. I must address Scott.

"Scott, would you please keep your hands to yourself. I know you are handsome and you are not used to no, but I'm dating someone, and that little thing you just did was too comfortable. We are not that close," I say, giving him a raised brow to let him know I'm serious.

"Oh, Cess, don't be so uptight, your hair fell in your face. I was merely trying to help you," Scott says, giving me that winning smile, and I couldn't help but smile back. Scott is such a flirt, maybe it's Draken who's making me all conscious about a man touching me.

"Okay Scott, just don't let it happen again," I shove him, in a playful manner. That is when I hear a growl. What is that noise? There were no signs about construction on campus.

"Did you all just hear that?" I ask, everyone shaking his and her head no. I hear it, again. Whoa, what is that? I'm going crazy. It reminds me of that dream with the dragon I had months ago. I've never been able to shake that dream, and what connection does Draken have with it? I feel very uneasy right now, like danger is coming.

"Is there work being done on school grounds, like remodeling, that would make a loud noise?"

"Cess, you are just nervous about the test, there is no remodeling going on," Linda says, shaking her head. I know what I hear. It's getting close. Why do I sense Draken is near? This is really creepy. I feel like I'm in a horror movie and something bad is about to happen. The door opens slowly, and in walk Draken,

Showken, and Layern. Holy shit, I did sense him. He is glaring at me.

"Draken, umm, what's wrong?" I ask, not getting a response, just a very slow walk over to me. He picks up my books, and starts placing them in my bag. I should say something, but not when he is like this. I better wait until he is calm. He would never harm me, would he? Everyone is looking at them. Rachel is looking at Showken, and to my surprise, so is Linda.

"Cess, do you know this guy grabbing your things? We have not even started studying," Scott says, and is thrown across the room. It's like everything is in slow motion. Showken and Layern are calming everyone, saying it's just a misunderstanding, and Scott is over in the corner, bleeding from the mouth. I look up at Draken, who has his hand out for me. I'm not taking it. He is crazy.

"I'm not going anywhere, why are you here, and why did you just do that to Scott?" I ask, pissed, but not yelling. Draken looks very scary right now. Linda and Kyle go over to Scott, he is yelling at Draken now.

"You are going to jail, you are finished! I don't know what your problem is, but when I'm done with you, you'll wish you were dead!"

"Dead is what you will be if you speak another word to me," Draken says, with a coldness that I've never heard. "Showken, Layern, take care of this. Princess and I are leaving." When I start to protest he grabs my arm, pulling, standing me up and walking me out of the room. When he closes the door I can't hear anything that was going on in the room. What did he mean, for his brother to take care of it? Draken and his brother are not into killing, are they? I mean, they are from another country. Shit, I have gotten myself into something now. I'm not sure if I should be scared or pissed at being pulled down the hall as he is scanning the rooms. He finally settles on one, opening the door and closing it behind him. There are no windows in this room. I feel an ache in my side, and the roar is getting louder.

"Draken, you, have you lost your mind? I'm not scared of you! Let me out of here! Why did you do that to him, and how did you even find me?" I yell.

"Princess, please be quiet, for your safety," he says, through clenched teeth. His head is down, and he won't look at me.

"I'm leaving."

"DON'T MOVE!" he yells. Oh shit, I need to pee. I'm scared. What is happening? Have I been sleeping with a crazy man? I've been sleeping with a crazy man.

"Draken."

"Did I not say be quiet?"

"What did I do?" I'm confused about why he is here like this.

"I told you, I warned you, yet you still did it anyway."

"Did what? I did nothing at all, we are just studying."

"He touched you. More importantly, you touched him back,

smiling. Why?"

"Draken, you are over-reacting- wait, how did you know that?"

"You have forced my hand, Princess, I can't take another man touching YOUUUU!" He still doesn't look up, but is pacing in front of the door. I want to leave and check on everyone.

"Are my friends okay?" I ask quietly. He snarls.

"Yes, they will never know any of this took place."

"What? Draken, what are you taking about? You threw Scott across the room. There was blood running from his mouth. I can't be with you if you are violent. Wait, you still haven't said how you knew what happened," I say, trying to get him to look at me, I bend trying to see his face, but he turns quickly, grabbing me and pinning me to the wall. He presses his head into my chest and roars.

"Draken, you are scaring me now, what is going on?" I ask, afraid.

"You forced me, Princess, I'm not someone you can take my requests and do as you please."

"Draken, I need to know everything."

"You will, I have no choice now, but I need you right now," he says, and I can hear his breathing calming. I'm not having sex right now.

"Princess, I need you so I can gain control, you are the only one who can help me. I'll explain, I promise, even how I knew how to find you and how I'd seen everything, just let me make love to you right now." Whoa, he has never said that to me. Make love? Whether he loves me or not, this outburst is unacceptable.

"Draken, I don't think . . . it's not a good time, we need to talk."

"I said we will, please don't deny me Princess, I smell your arousal," he says, taking a deep breath. I close my eyes, trying to think. I feel him holding my hands above my head and using his other hand to stroke down my side, squeezing my breast.

"Draken, please," I say, as my body starts to submit to his hands.

"Please what?"

"Draken, this is not the time. We really, ohhh, noo!" He gently slips two fingers inside me, twisting and turning, and doing it torturously slow, in . . . out . . . in . . . out, and before I can think straight, I agree.

"Okay, Draken,"

"Princess, I-" he starts to speak, but he lets go of my hands and hikes me up, placing my legs around his waist. My clothes are gone, and before I can change my mind, Draken is inside me, thrusting. He is very gentle, and is kissing me everywhere like he had lost me.

"You're going to hate me, but I don't want you to. I have to tell you now," he whispers into my ear, biting and licking my ear lobe.

"Draken, I just need, ooh, talk."

"Mmm, Princess, don't. Just feel me, my body, my strength, my weakness and my beast," he says, and I'm lost in his words. I can't believe this is happening. When we are done, he pulls out of me gently, not letting my legs go. I hold on as he fixes his clothes and places me on a counter. Without speaking, Draken pulls my shorts back on and I notice my panties are in shreds, but he places them in his pants pocket.

"Come. I need to face the music." We walk out the door where Showken and Layern are, not making eye contact, and stand outside his SUV. I climb in and he follows. The ride is silent, and I feel his pain as he sits next to me, looking out the window. We pull into their driveway, and he is out of the car and around to my side, opening the door before I can turn my head.

"Draken, if you don't start talking now, I'm going home."

"I will explain, but not outside, please just let me get it out," he says, and I notice Showken and Layern look serious, but hurt also. What is going on?

"Fine," I snap, feeling very confused. I've just seen and heard some crazy shit, yet my stupid body submits to him. I walk into the house, where Hawken and Gemi are standing, no one is saying anything. They look like someone has died or something. I'm not moving until I get some answers. I'm standing in the foyer as Draken comes and stands before me.

"Princess."

"Don't call me that. How did you know where I was and what happened? Are you watching me? Have a listening device on me? What? Because I really need some answers right now."

"I was not supposed to fall in love with you, but I did. You were chosen by me to be a Giver for me. I know you don't know what that is, but just listen. As the relationship grew, I found myself needing to be around you. See . . . Layern has a gift . . . and I can find you by your scent, because I carry it with me, now. This is new to me and I told you, no touching, and you touched and he touched. I need to be where you are. Also, my thoughts are not logical when it comes to you."

"Draken, you are talking in circles." I say, placing my hands on my hips. "Just tell me the truth without the incomplete thoughts. You are skipping the growling I heard, and you tossed Scott fifteen feet," I'm a little shaky because I think he just admitted to loving me, but I'm not sure. Shit, I'm not sure of anything right now.

"Look, I'm trying to give you answers without terrifying you, too. I'm not letting you go, so you can get that out of your head. I thought I could let you go, but I'm not willing to - what the fuck!" Draken says, with a hissing sound. I turn and see a beautiful woman coming down the hallway. This better be one of his brothers' women, or I'm so done with him. "Ravla, why are you here?" Oh, so he knows her.

"I was concerned, Draken, you hadn't called for me. So I came to make sure you were being taken care of," the woman says, looking at me with a frown.

"Ravla, you lie!" Layern says, as Draken turns extremely scary-looking.

"Draken, who is this woman?" I turn and look at him.

"Oh, I'm his Giver. And you are?" she asks. I feel the need to say something, until Draken gets in her face.

"RAVLA!" Draken roars and everyone, including me, steps back. She is on her own, I don't know what is going on with them, but Draken is pissed and even his brothers feel it. Showken pulls me away from Draken.

"Draken, please, I was thinking," she says, glancing at me, and then looking at him. "Well, I figured you . . . uhh, didn't want me anymore, and I had to find out who you were seeing before you get married." Did she just say married?

"Married?" I say, looking at him. He doesn't look at me, but in a flash he moves his hand, and a purple glow is around her neck. When he turns to look at me, his face looks similar to the beast in my dream. I need to scream and my mouth is open, but nothing comes out. Everything goes dark.

DRAKEN

"You knew what you were doing, Ravla. I will never have you again, and you are bound to a cave until I decide your fate," I say, picking Princess up off the floor. She has passed out.

"Draken, please."

"It's Prince Draken to you from now on," I growl. Instantly two guards show up beside Ravla. I'm sure Showken sent for them. They open a portal, and her cries are nothing to me, as she has hurt my Princess to the core. "Layern, is she okay?"

"Yes, Draken, carry her to the study and lay her on the sofa."

"I've really fucked up now. She knows about my engagement. She will never forgive me, and I will never let her go," I say, walking quickly to lay her down. I don't even know how long she will be out. "Not to mention, I still need to tell her I'm a dragon. FUCK!"

"Draken, you just placed Ravla, your long time Giver, under arrest. You know you must go back and deal with that," Gemi says, looking me in the eye. One thing I can say about Gemi, he doesn't say much, but when he does he's usually right. Knowing protocol, I should be home meting out Ravla's punishment, but I can't leave Princess, she needs me.

"I will wake her now, she can't leave this house. Understand?" I ask everyone. They all nod, knowing she knows way too much for things to go back to being normal. I lean over and go into Princess' mind, urging her to wake. Her eyes are open in no time.

"Oh, Draken, I had the worst nightmare ever. I was at the school studying when . . ." she stops and looks around, noticing all my brothers are watching her very closely. "Shit, it wasn't a dream, you . . . you are a monster!"

"I'm a dragon, big difference," I say, watching as she curls up at the end of the couch. She looks so frightened. How could I let this happen?

"Are you all, umm, dragons?"

"Yes," Showken says, giving a winning smile. Only Showken would be smiling when I'm falling. Ravla exposed my marriage, which should never have been done. I exposed myself, by tracking her down when that human placed his hands in her hair, it was like I felt his filthy touch. She is looking at me with tears in her eyes.

"You mean I love a dragon?"

"You love me?" I ask, watching her expression.

"I thought you were a man. I'm scared, I want to go home, please."

"I can't allow that, Princess, I must talk with you first."

"Are you going to kill me?" Those words hurt more than anything I've ever heard. How could she think I would harm her, ever?

"No." That's all I can get out of my mouth. I'm so confused right now. I'm sure a messenger will be coming soon for me to go back to my land, leaving Princess with her thoughts. I can't take her home. I'm in so deep, and I can release her from me and me from her, but there is only one way.

"Princess, I-"

"Wait, are you getting married? Who was that lady? What . . . I need to go home. You can have this mess," Princess says, but Layern sends me her true feelings and she is really hurting, her heart is broken. She really does love me.

"Yes, and no. I'm scheduled to be married, but I'm cancelling it. I love you, Princess, and I want you, I want you to choose me," I say, begging. Who would have thought I would be begging a human to choose me?

"I . . . choose you? I did choose you, but you're engaged, and you still have not said who that other woman is. I guess cheating on me is what guys do. I give you my heart and you do me like

Travis. D told me it was too soon, not to mention you are a dragon."

"Please, Princess."

"Are you holding me captive, or can I go home? Don't worry, it's too embarrassing to say I fell in love with a dragon man who is married and obviously has women on the side. You disgust me," she says, letting the tears roll down her face. I look at my brothers. I will let her think she's home, creating a fake image when she leaves. I'm too hurt to get enough power to do it. I need to go handle Ravla, and protest this marriage. I will go visit Princess in her mind until it's all sorted out. I think the best thing, now, is to make her think she is at home, and I'll handle my world. If she chooses to leave me, then I have to take the only option left to me, death.

"Okay, okay, you can go home." I look at Showken and he nods, letting me know it's done. Now, when Princess goes home, it will be the same, only it's not real. She rises very slowly and backs away from me, and I feel my heart being ripped out. She's still crying, and as soon as she leaves, I hear her running out the door. I close my eyes and tears flow down. I have never cried in my life. If I can't have Princess, death is what I want. I walk into my bedroom and pack all that I have, opening the portal and leaving for home, never to return.

***

Walking to my room, passing servants who are bowing and speaking kind words, assures me of my being home. I place my things in order and go to the garden, where I find my mother in her favorite place in the castle.

"Queen Nala, Mother of Draglen Descendants, permission to speak," I ask, looking around my land and seeing other dragons flying freely. Everything is so beautiful and free, yet I feel ugly and trapped.

"My son, please come," my mother opens her arms and I walk into her arms for comfort. She holds me, knowing the decision I have made, and I hear her sob.

"Mother, don't cry, please."

"Just marry your wife to be, my son, don't do this, please. My heart will rip a thousand times." I pull back and see my mother's face. She is beautiful. I can't stop her pain, because everything rests on Princess choosing me.

"My heart is ripping right now, mother. I love her, and she may not want me because of what I am, and if she can't, I won't live without her."

"Bring her, then, son, I will accept her. I can't lose my son, the heir to this throne. The land will be in chaos, making us vulnerable, it can subject us to other lands trying to come and take ours."

"I won't force her; I will try to convince her. I do have to decide on a punishment for Ravla, she should never have showed up without my sending for her."

"You do what you must to Ravla, just remember, she is probably hurt, too. She has always loved you," my mother says, rubbing my hair. When she rubs my hair I feel so much better, usually, but today, I feel worse.

"I will, mother." I nod, and walk across the garden, heading for the caves where Ravla waits for her punishment. I am close when I see the sorrow birds following me. I guess they sense my feelings. I get to the gate where Ravla is, and I see her pacing. There are two of the guardians outside her gate. She is frightened when she sees me coming. I will not show one ounce of mercy with Ravla, she disobeyed the rules.

"Ravla, why did you come?" I ask, folding my arms across my chest.

"Dra . . . Prince Draken, I was concerned for your sexual needs. Plus I, I needed you, too. You know I'm not allowed to touch another, being your Giver."

"YOUR NEEDS ARE NOT MY CONCERN, RAVLA! YOU! ARE! A! GIVER! NOTHING MORE!" I yell, and feel the ground shake. I see the sky clear from happy flyers to very frightened dragons. I glance back at the guardians and they are nervous. I forgot my voice makes people scared. Ravla starts backing up against the wall, and her eyes are changing from human to dragon form. I don't give a fuck.

"You will stay here until I decide your punishment, and you

are not allowed to transform into your dragon until I say, or that around your neck will choke you to death before you can stretch your wings," I say. I turn and walk away. I hear her cries. I'm hurting, too. She will be let loose if I die, anyway. I close my eyes, transforming into my beast, and take off into the sky. Our sky changes colors every few seconds, forming a great show all the time. I take my time sweeping the land. My people are so happy, dancing and playing music. I fly past a group of Youngs trying to learn how to fly high. Finally, I come upon my father, on the cliff of Hulin. I land next to him and he is in human form, yet I bow my head waiting to hear him talk.

"Draken my son, heir to the throne, why do you break my heart? You mother told you to end it with that human, now you're in love, you say. I'm glad you are in your true form, but I don't want to hear you speak. I'm angry, because you are choosing her over your family. She should not be this important, son, only if . . . is she the Key?" I nod, meeting my father's gaze. I know he understands. A Key is rare, and only a few have ever found one, but it's when a dragon shifter's true love is human. It has to happen to keep the portal open to travel back and forth. The human can then be allowed into the land. "Who else knows this? Oh, you're in dragon form, shift." I quickly shift into human, getting ready to do an official introduction, but my father stops me.

"Draken, speak freely."

"Well, Father, yes, I think she is my Key, I can't live without her. I can sense her even in our land. I miss her now, and want her so badly. I want her with me every night. I won't live without her."

"I won't ask you to. You need to convince her, son. I don't want to lose you, and I'm sure your brothers will not be happy, as it will involve them."

"I will do my best, Father. I just don't know where to start."

"She is a woman, son. Do what any beast, man, or other would do. Agree with whatever she wants, say yes to whatever she wants, and most of all, make sure she can't walk when you're done pleasing her."

"Thanks, Dad. I'm going to go lie in my bed and go see my Princess in her mind. I need to comfort her, I can feel her tears and I hate that I'm the cause of it. I just hope she will be able to look past me being a dragon," I say.

"I hope for your sake she does, too." I vanish, ending up lying on my bed. I close my eyes, going to comfort my Princess. I feel her pain as I get close.

I find her in bed, crying. I call her name, "Princess."

"Draken?"

"Yes, Princess, talk to me, tell me what you are thinking."

"How are you communicating with me?"

"I can communicate with you because I'm connected to you."

"So you're not really here?"

"Princess, I'm here for you, always."

"I mean you're in my head, right?" She is making this so hard.

She has curled her body into a fetal position, I don't want to scare her, but here it goes. I want her to feel me. I slide into her bed. In her mind I'm really in her room, it's just another advantage. I get right behind her, placing my hand on her waist. "Draken," she cries harder.

"Princess, yes, I'm here. I'm sorry you are hurting, but I'm not sorry for loving you. I need you, Princess, please, come share my world with me."

"Draken, I love you, but you lied. You're getting married, and most important, you're a dragon." I move in close, getting right up to her ear.

"I never lied, Princess, and I'm not marrying anybody if it can't be you."

"Draken, just leave and go have your life, I will never be the same."

"Why?"

"How could I fall for a guy who loves another?"

"Princess, I love you, and no-one else. That bride was chosen for me before I could fly." She tries to turn, but I hold her tighter. I want her every night.

"So, you're a dragon?"

"Yes, I am."

"Can you shoot fire from your mouth?" I hope she gets all her questions out. Many things about my people are myths. We live in harmony among one another.

"Yes, I can shoot fire from my mouth, hands, eyes, and if I get really angry, my entire body can become fire without burning." I feel her tense up as I'm talking. I have to assure her I would never harm her. "I don't have to use those abilities most of the time. Because I'm a prince, most of the time I'm working to ensure peace in our land. We don't fight, only with other lands, never among each other. Except me and my brothers, we fight sometimes." I say. I want to be inside her so badly, but I can't, she needs to know me.

"Draken, how can this be, you being a dragon? I mean, I was taught you are bad, evil and ugly. I don't know how this will work. My family is not going to want me with a dragon. Where is your land? Do you live here on earth?" My father's words come back into my thoughts, and I don't hold back.

"My land is called Cortamagen, and it's in another realm, very far from Earth. We use a portal to travel back and forth. We come to Earth because we do business here, and one myth is right, we like treasure, so we are always hunting for it. I'm not evil at all, Princess, I'm in love, with you," I say, placing a feather kiss on her shoulder. I feel her shiver. She still wants me.

"Draken, please."

"Please, what?"

"I can't do this with you." It feels like I'm being stabbed over and over, in the same wound. I close my eyes. I know she wants me. It's her ideas of dragons that have her mind all crazy.

"Draken, the dream, was that you?"

"Yes, that was me."

"So, that is you, the dragon."

"Yes, that's my other, my beast, and he loves you, too."

"Please don't say that."

"Okay, I'm sorry. I know this is all new and you need time." I swallow hard, wanting her so badly it is killing me.

"Who is that woman?"

"A jealous woman I used to sleep with."

"You mean have sex, right?"

"Yes, that is what we did, but it was more like passing time. It meant nothing to me." This is not turning out good. She asking about Ravla, I swear if I die so will Ravla. I will not let her live if she is the cause of my losing Princess.

"She's very pretty, why don't you want her?"

"Fuck her. She's nothing compared to you. You're the most beautiful woman I know, and I love you," I say, wishing I could just go this very moment and choke the shit out of Ravla. I thought she had more class than to do what she did, but I guess not.

"Draken, I can't be with you, this is why I'm hurting so bad. I love you and you're not even human. I can't travel back and forth to different realms, I mean, what do I tell my parents about me being gone and they can't call? If I was to be with you, what if I get pregnant? I mean, can you even get me pregnant?" These questions are driving me crazy, but she's my Key, and if my father is right, then I just keep her talking until I can get her to come home with me.

"You would always be able to communicate with your parents and your brother. Others, I'm not sure. I could find out, though. As for children, I want to have lots of babies with you. I've done my research, they would be like me, shifters, my gene would overpower yours."

"What? Draken." I begin rubbing her hip, slowly, in a circle. She moans "Ah, mmm."

"Princess, I want you in my life, I need you in my life, I can't have one without you, and I refuse a life without you." I smell her arousal, and now I'm as hard as a rock.

"Draken, I have to think. This is really hard for me. I don't know what to think right now, and you touching me is making me lose my logic."

"I want you to stop trying to convince yourself, Princess. I love you, please, say you love me, too."

"I do love you, Draken, but I'm not sure who you are, or if this is some sick trick that is being played on me. I want you, in this world. I would not fit in your world. I'm just me, not anything special."

"You will be if you say yes."

"What does that mean? I'll become a dragon?"

"No, that is a birthright, but I will share myself with you, which gives you more than some dragons," I say, wanting to show her, but I can't until she is mine.

"I won't lie and say that I'm not curious, I-" She breaks down and starts crying again. I hate her crying. It feels like I'm being pulled apart.

"Please, Princess, your crying is ripping me apart."

"I know this is not what you want to hear, but I won't leave with you, Draken, I love you so much, but my brother, he's my twin. If I leave it will tear us both apart. My brother gets me when nobody else does. D would not be right if he could not be around me. I would have to keep secrets, I'm sure, and I can't, if it was just seeing my parents every now and again, maybe, but D, no I won't leave him, not even for you, Draken." She's made her decision no. This can't be happening. I can't live without her. She's my air. I won't breathe if Princess leaves me. I will die. I want to die if she won't accept me.

"Princess, just think about it, don't decide now," I beg. I feel like everything is closing in on me.

"Draken, you're a dragon, you live on another planet. I could never understand this between us."

"Princess, please don't. Listen, we don't have to rush, we could wait until you are ready to make the final move."

"Final move?" Shit, I forgot, once she comes with me she could never come back to earth, again.

"Yes, Princess, I won't lie. If you decide to come with me and be my wella, or as you would say, my wife, you can never return to earth," I say, feeling like shit for asking her to give up her family for me.

"What? I can't, Draken. You're asking me to give up my entire life and go to a place I've never been. What if I don't like it when I get there? What if your land hates me?"

"I know it's selfish of me, and I promise to dedicate each day of my life to you, and I will even work on a way you can travel back. But yes, I want you with me forever."

"You have to give me time, Draken, but right now my answer is no. I won't leave D, my parents, and my friends for you. You tricked me and you're getting married, that's why only six months. Yes, I've been thinking, you knew this between us would never work, that is why you said six months. Well, let's just end it sooner. Please go, and let me cry."

"I will leave now, Princess, but I won't ever let you go," I say, returning to my bed, looking at my gold ceiling. I can't marry another when I love Princess. I will let the family know and let my father cancel the ceremony. I can't keep Princess in an image of her house. I will call Showken and have him place her in her home for real. I will not take that away from her. I should never have thought I could have her; she's a precious gift to the universe. I walk out of my room and make the arrangements that I need. I will not live without her.

CESS

He's a dragon. I've been having sex with a dragon. I'm in love with a dragon. This is the twilight zone. I just know this can't be real. Who the hell would believe me? If I just could have stuck with my plan. I drag myself out of bed, heading for the bathroom. Draken should never have come to talk with me. He asks me to leave my family. I need a shower, to cry. As I walk into the bathroom I look in the mirror, only to see flashes of my dream coming back.

He must have been trying to tell me then. I climb into the shower and shock my body to life with the water, letting it warm from cold to hot. I need this, and my tears won't stop. How can I choose? When I'm done, I stagger out of my room, dragging myself to my closet, and put on a sundress. I head to my dance room and crank up the music, dancing my pain away. I will never stop loving him. I dance, it seems for hours, and when I curl up on the floor I'm dripping with sweat. I hear footsteps. I can't see Draken again.

"Hey Cess, don't tense up, it's just me coming in," I recognize this voice; it's Showken, who is also a dragon.

"Please leave, I don't want to talk," I say, turning onto my belly. I fill tears forming again. I can't keep crying. It's over.

"Cess, do you love my brother, forget that he's a dragon. Just, do you love him?"

"Showken, yes, I love him, but he is a dragon and so are you, so leave."

"Cess, you need to decide and make it fast. I hate to see my brother in pain. Cess, you can't just walk away like this. You belong with Draken. The sooner you accept this, the better it will be for both of you."

"Showken, I can't leave my family, you're asking me to give up something that I can't."

"My brother is making a sacrifice for you, get your shit together and come to my land."

"Fuck youuuuu!" I yell. "I don't and will not do anything you or anyone says. This is my decision and I've made it. I'm staying in my own land." I stand to look him in the eye. He glares back, and then gives me a huge smile.

"You and Draken are a lot alike, he, too, gets pissed like you, but Cess, I will tell you what others won't. You are connected to my brother, and soon, because of all the physical activity, you will look different."

"What? You're kidding right. I mean not like a dragon?"

"No, that is our birthright, but you will gain something, Cess, just come with me. Please?"

"You have to be kidding me, my family, you asshole, I will not leave them wondering if I'm dead. You are just as selfish as Draken, get the fuck out of my house."

"Nope."

"What?"

"I said no, Cess, my brother has made it known to my family that he wants to die if he can't have you." I can't believe my ears. Did he just say die?

"You mean Draken is going to kill himself? Over me? He should marry his fiancée, and that other woman wants him, too, so his options are wide," I snap. They want to give me a bag of bricks like I caused this. He knew better, I thought he was human, he led me on and now I should feel sorry? What about me? My feelings don't count?

"I mean, we would have to kill him, and I can't kill my brother. If Draken wants to die all the siblings must circle him and burn him all at the same time, sending out our most intense fire. I can't do that, and if I have to throw you over my shoulder, I will. I will not kill my brother, not for him, you, or even the law of my land," Showken says, with a seriousness I've never seen in him before. I look close and he is teary-eyed. I don't want Draken to die, but if I leave, my mother and father will be hurt, but my brother would die, also. He is my twin, my best friend, and if I vanish, so will he, in his mind. I'm not going to let Showken bully me.

"Draken doesn't know you're here. You will not drag me because he won't allow that, I know that much after the thing with Scott, and I love Draken, but you will not trick me with the lame excuse he is going to kill himself."

"Lame, Cess, get real, I'm not lying to you. In fact, I was the one who said "date my brother for six months, have a good time". You fell in love, and so did he. Now, I will give you time to think, and you're home now by the way."

"I've been home for a while now. What are you talking about, Showken?"

"Cess, I'll never tell. Be back after your final tomorrow."

"Bye, Showken, and I'll call you."

"See you tomorrow, Cess," Showken says, both brows arched. He looks as if nothing I say can ease his pain, he will be by again with that "Draken is going to kill himself." Draken would not do that? Oh wait, his brothers would kill him, yeah right. I'm not falling for that bunch of bull crap. He would not give up everything for me. I hate Showken for even saying that. There is no way . . . would he? I mean, I feel strongly about Draken; I love him, very much, but give up my life? I wouldn't do that. He would leave his parents, brothers, land, and business all for me. I hate that I love you, Draken. Now, I have to think. I need to take my final tomorrow, that I didn't get a chance to study for, and I don't think I can with these thoughts. I need to talk with D. I go on the hunt for my twin. I need him right now. I can't tell him the truth, but I could get some sort of advice. I find D in the media room, watching one of his favorite movies. I go in and take a seat next to him. I put my hand in his popcorn, shoving a handful into my mouth, thinking I might as well watch with him. D will not stop watching

"Once Upon A Time in Mexico," he doesn't want anyone to know this, but I do. I sit and laugh at the movie with D, eating popcorn and sharing his soda. I realize, never doing this again with my twin is too much to ask. I love my brother, heck, we shared a womb. I don't think Draken understands this. I can't tell D that I'm leaving to be with my dragon boyfriend in a place I know nothing about. That's freaking crazy. D stops the credits and turns the lights on, coming back to sit with me.

"So, what's got you all confused, sis?" He knows me so well. Oh D, I want to tell you everything, but you will think I'm crazy, and you would make sure I saw the best therapist money could buy. I have to do this right without tipping him off, telling part-truths and leaving out some parts.

"Draken wants to take the relationship to another level, and I don't know if I can do it, or even if I want to," I say.

"Sis, you want to. It's all over your face every time you say his name, or when you are around him. It's like looking at a very happy love movie, with you starring. So, what are you waiting for?"

"He wants me to move in with him and I just don't want that, plus he's not from here," I say, really trying to be cautious with my words. It is so hard not to tell D the truth. We always tell each other the truth, no matter what.

"Okay, so he leaves for another country, Cess. You know I would come see you, this guy loves you, I was suspicious of him at first, but he is truly a good guy, and good for you. Besides, anybody can keep you smiling like that all the time, I say keep him."

"D, I'm young and just finishing school, I'm not sure, but I think Draken wants marriage and I'm not ready for that. I mean, what if I never see you again because you're working and I'm somewhere else." I'm trying to keep from saying I would never see you again, but the words won't come out. Then I would have to say he's a dragon in another land, not earth, which would lead me back to I'm crazy. Where the hell do they think Draken goes when he is not in the business world? Oh, Mom did say it's been rumored he owns islands, so that would explain that.

"Cess, you should go with your heart, if I'm ever that lucky to meet someone I love and they want me for me, not money or our name Lamil, I'm going to marry her before someone else gets a chance. Listen, we are always going to be able to communicate with each other, even if we don't see each other every day." I begin to let the tears fall " Don't cry, sis, I want you happy. Never give up being with the one you love for me, or anyone. Sometimes love only comes once in a lifetime, and you will be kicking yourself forever if you let him go, never to meet another like him."

"I'm sure I won't meet another man like Draken, ever. I just . . . just don't know, D. This is such a huge commitment and change for me. You really think Draken loves me that much?" I say, looking into my brother's eyes and seeing the truth. He begins to wipe my face with his hand, and kisses my cheek, which makes me cry harder.

"I'm always going to be your brother, and no amount of distance can change that, Cess, not ever."

"I love you, D. Thank you for talking with me." I sniff into his shoulder. "Thanks for letting me watch your favorite movie, which I will still never tell."

"I know, sis, I know." D and I stay like this for a few more minutes, then he puts on another movie to watch, another good one, "Gladiator." Russell Crowe can always cheer me up. We talk through the movie, saying what we would have done if we were in that story. These are the times I would miss. D has given me something to think about, but right now, I will enjoy my brother and Russell Crowe. I smile, and start on some more popcorn.

***

Finally, I'm done with school. That was a very hard exam. My parents, D and I are going to dinner tonight to celebrate. D and I are college graduates. My dad asked was Draken coming, but I told him he was out of town. I could not stand to sit at a table with Draken, knowing what I know about him. He is getting married, supposedly he cancelled, someone showed up like they are very familiar with one another, and he is a dragon. Which I could maybe get over, I'm still debating, but those women, that is a hard pill to swallow. Then thinking of D talking with me, I realize I do love Draken, and I think he loves me, too. I try to enjoy our time out, but I can't focus on anything but Draken's voice asking me to be with him. Then Showken comes and says he is going to die. I'm not sure if he is telling the truth or not. Finally I hear my father's voice.

"Princess, where is your mind at? I called your name three times," my father says.

"Maybe if you said "Cess," I would have heard," I say, out loud, but meaning to say in my head.

"What did you just say?" my father asks, in that no-nonsense tone.

"I'm sorry, Dad, just been thinking a lot." I look up, giving him my "sorry" face.

"Okay, I understand. Draken said you guys have been

discussing big issues between you two."

"WHAT!" I yell. My mother nods her head in approval and smiles very sweetly at me. What the hell? When did this happen? "I mean, Dad, when did you talk with Draken?"

"This morning, Princess, and I've already said yes."

"Yes to what?" I'm in shock right now, I can't believe this is turning out this way. How did he talk with my father and not me? Well, I did say I wanted to be alone, but still.

"Darling, I think your father is trying to say, Draken asked for your hand in marriage and we both said yes. I'm so happy for you, I can't believe my daughter is marrying Draken Draglen, I couldn't have picked better," my mother says, gleefully. I can't believe this, he asked my parents if he could marry me and did not ask me. This keeps getting better. I bet he didn't tell them he is a dragon and he wants me in another land I've never heard of, or the fact I could never see them again.

"I'm speechless, well, I need a glass of wine," I say.

"Yes, let's have a toast to my two wonderful kids and to your engagement." my father signals the waiter.

"Wait, I've not been asked for marriage, and who said I would say yes?" I say, frowning at my father and mother. D keeps eating, a smirk on his face. Shit, he knew, too. Everyone has secrets from me. I can't believe this is happening.

"Of course you will say yes, Princess, why would you say no?" my mother says, frowning slightly. "Besides, I've already reserved the country club for a few Saturdays, you can choose which one, of course," she smiles again. Well, fuck me. They all seem to think this is okay, just to give me away. My mother thinks he is a dream come true. Well, he is a dream come true. He loves me so gently. He talks with me, getting to know me, and he loves me. Why would he talk with my father and not me, though?

"D, you are pretty quiet. What do you think about your sister getting married?" my father asks. D finally looks up and stares me right in the eye.

"I think Cess should be happy, and if he makes her happy, I'm happy." D says. "Cess and I've already talked. She knows what I think, and she knows we will always be twins, and no distance will ever separate us," My eyes water again. D's opinion is so important to me. I can't bear to think of never being able to see his handsome face again, eating my food and making fun of me. I love the bond he and I share.

"Princess, I would not say yes if I didn't think Draken was a good catch. I love you, and you two have been inseparable for the last few months. I thought naturally you would want to. I mean, Draken is a little older, but not by much. You had to know he would want a wife," my father says, while we all get a refill.

"Well, I thought I would have been asked first."

"Nonsense, Draken knows tradition. It's respectable to ask the father before asking the daughter. What if he asked you and I said no, then he'd be up shit creek." He holds up his glass. "Now, lets have a toast." I hesitantly hold my glass as my father begins his toast. I start to think of my time with Draken, being in the kitchen cooking with him, dancing together, walking around in the park. Laughing at Showken's lame jokes was always a part of all our time together. Then, my mind drifts to all our sexual times together, and how he ran bath water for me, carrying me to the tub to soak and relax, such awesome times. I finally hear my father say, "To my Princess and her future husband." We touch glasses and I sip my wine, feeling the need to run away to think. Could I leave and go be with Draken? Is it even possible to be with him? I'm not sure, I just can't wait to get home. There is more talking to my mother about the wedding, and my father talking to D about his position at the company. I sit in a daze. I can't wait to get home. Finally, my father is done, and we go to the car where my father's driver, Jimmy, is waiting for us. We climb in and head for home. When we turn onto our street, and I see Draken's house come into view, my heart beats a little faster and my hands become hot. I miss him. Draken is my heart, I love him so.

When we all get inside I walk to my room, where I have been kind of hoping I would see him waiting for me, as he often does. Now, I know he could get in easily because he has powers that allow him in without being seen. I get out of my dress and head for the shower, and then I smell him.

"Draken?" I look around and don't see anyone, yet I know he is here. "Draken, just come out and talk with me," I say out loud.

Still there's no response. "This is not funny, I'm saying I will talk with you, I mean you have talked with my parents, asked for my hand in marriage and never asked me." I look around my room, under my bed, in the closet and still no response. "Answer me, damn it. I don't have time for you and your dragon tricks." That's when I hear a growl. Shit, he must be sensitive about the dragon thing.

"Okay, sorry about that, but no need to growl at me, Draken, you don't have to hide." I wait a few more minutes. I go into the bathroom and start my shower. As the steam fogs the mirror, I see on it, "Princess, I love you, Draken." Oh shit, he is here, or was.

"I love you, too, Draken, but love is not our problem, and you know this," I say out loud, hoping he can hear me. I take my shower, and put on a nightshirt. I climb into bed, hoping to get a visit from Draken, but nothing. I cry all night. He is not letting me think and make the decision, he has already asked for my hand. I mean, he is still that ass I met on the first day. I still can't believe he walked me off the property, now he is begging me to be with him. I will go to his house first thing in the morning and demand that one of his brothers go get him. For one, so I can prove Showken is a liar, and two, so I can chew him out about this entire situation. The morning is not going to come fast enough.

***

Finally the house is empty. I put on my clothes and head to Draken's house. It feels like it was just yesterday. I wanted to see who was moving in. If I had listened to D, I would not be in a situation where I have to choose. Then, I would never have met Draken, and though he is an ass, and has got me into a hell of a predicament, I still love him. I make it to the door and start ringing the doorbell. I know someone is here. I wait and no one shows; I try the door, and it opens. I go in, yelling out Draken's name. There are boxes everywhere. I guess they're leaving with Draken.

"Draken, we need to talk," I yell, heading for his room. I know he hears me, I hear a growl and it frightens me. Shit, maybe this was a bad idea. I move faster, I will feel safer in Draken's room. I'm too far into the house to make a run for the door. I close the door when I get into his room, and call his name again. "Draken!" I yell. "I think one of your brothers is trying to scare me, or should I say has scared me, please Draken, I'm scared!" I hear the growl, and it's his growl. It's loud, like he is giving a command. "Thanks Draken, I know that was you, you told them not to scare me, didn't you?" I see his bed and my body heats up, remembering all our lovemaking in this bed, the floor, his chair, against the wall, yes, that was really fun. I sit on his bed, lie back and began to cry. "Draken, why won't you answer me? I know I said I can't leave my family, but I don't hate you." The door opens.

"Draken?"

"No, Showken. Are you here to be with my brother?"

"Showken, was that you growling at me, you scared me. I want to talk with Draken."

"Yes, it was me, Cess, sorry about that. I'm just pissed, but my brother corrected me. You can only see Draken if you accept-"

"Don't scare me again, and accept what?"

"Cess, stop playing dumb, the lifetime with Draken. Coming to my land is what I want to hear. Will you save Draken, or will you be a coward and let my brother die for you?" Showken says, unsmiling. He's serious.

"I want to speak with Draken, right now!"

"Okay, then you have to come to my land, that's the only way," he snaps. "I so want to hate you, but Draken made me promise, but if he dies, then so will you."

"What are you talking about? You're still talking about Draken dying? Showken, stop saying that!"

"It's true, he has already killed Ravla, because he feels she was the cause of your not wanting him, and he waits for his own death. I refuse to be a part of it, so my father has taken my place. I'm here to settle our business affairs. We will never return to this land again." He stares at me, and his eyes turn really green. I see that he is telling the truth. What have I done? I will do it, I will go. I can't let him die.

"Showken, take me to Draken, right now," I say, shaking. I'm not even dressed for this. Shit. I should have worn something other than shorts and a shirt.

"You serious?"

"Yes, let's go before I change my mind. You better be telling the truth, or I'm going to kick your dragon ass and still find a way home. I'm not saying I will be with Draken, I just don't want him doing anything for me." Showken picks me up and starts swinging me around. I hear the growl and so does he. He puts me down fast.

"Sorry," he says, pulling out a round case about the size of a powder compact. He pulls me close and says, "hold on." It's like something out a movie, we are moving faster than anything. I'm screaming the entire time, knowing this was a bad idea. I can hear Draken's growl getting louder. Showken's face is turning green. Shit, it's his dragon. We finally make it, and I need to vomit. We end up outside some sort of huge stadium. I lean over and puke my guts out.

"Cess, come on, the ceremony is starting." Showken pulls me in through a door and it's beautiful, the walls shine with jewels of all different colors. I can hear a man talking, and his voice is commanding and scary. Showken continues to pull me along, and we enter the stadium. Draken is tied to a huge pole that looks like it's going to touch the sky, and he is in full dragon. That's why he can't talk, he is in dragon form. There are dragons around him in all colors, even one that looks crystal clear. Holy shit, he is going to die.

"Showken, what is happening?"

"I told you, they are going to burn him all at once, that is the only way."

"No, they won't!" I lose my mind, these things are like huge over me, I'm surrounded by dinosaurs. Showken is right with me. I begin yelling for everyone to stop, but that is when the fire starts to come from the dragons surrounding him. Oh no, I'm too late.

DRAKEN

"DRAAAKEN!!" She's here! I gather my strength and start firing back, but I'm weak. I'm not going to make it. When I see my brother, Showken, who would not stand, I'm pleased. He changes into a dragon, and starts hitting my other brothers with fire. Princess is screaming and crying. I need to go to her. I roar loudly. Showken is fighting with them, and my father stops burning me. I break free, the chains falling to the ground. I'm badly hurt. She does love me. I knew she loved me. My dragon is so weak. I can't protect her. Showken will do it, I see him standing in front of her.

"You killed him, you killed him, please Draken, don't die, I love you, I love you!"

Showken stands there protecting her from the others, humans

are not allowed in this arena. Please, Showken, protect my wella, keep her safe. Showken roars, causing some of my brothers to take a step back. Everyone thinks Showken is all smiles, but when he is dragon, he is all beast, and very deadly if he has to be.

"Showken, I need to get to Draken. Please, I need you to help me, don't let them harm me!" I see my mother coming towards Princess; she helps her from the ground. I feel Princess' hesitation.

"You are the one, the human who has my son's heart, no harm will come to you. I will make sure. Come, I'll take you to the center so you can see your prince."

"Okay." Princess shakes as she walks past the others, who snarl as she passes them. My mother corrects them.

"Do not dishonor me, children, my son's wella has come!" she says firmly, smiling at Princess. I growl as I smell her fear of this place. I will make her feel comfortable as soon as I get my strength. She comes close and begins to cry. I hate her crying.

"I love you, Draken. Please live," she says. I will live, Princess, I will, I say in my head.

"He says he will," my mother says, nudging her closer to me.

"He is hurt so bad, will he live?" Princess asks.

"You ask too many questions, go to your prince and reassure him," my mother says, pushing her forward. Each step she takes makes me happy my Princess came. She comes to me and begins rubbing my head.

"Draken, you are hurt so bad and you can't talk right now. I love you, Draken, and I'm so angry you would die on me like this. When you heal I'm going to kill you." She leans over, lays her hands on my huge neck and cries harder. I whimper in pain and joy, for I have my Princess. She is amazing, risking her life for me. I open my eyes, turning my beast head to see her. She looks at me with a smile that heals my heart instantly. I feel her hands exploring my dragon.

"Draken, they really were going to kill you. I'm not afraid of this, I mean your beast, it's very pretty." I huff a little, to let her know pretty is not want I want to hear. "Oh, you don't like pretty, well, I have no other way to explain it, so suck it up. The shades of purple are amazing. I can't wait till you heal, so I can really touch you," she says, and I can feel her love. I look at my brothers as they observe her, wondering. I'm sure now we have a human that will sit on the throne one day as Queen. My Father has shifted, and I sense his presence near Princess.

"Hello, my son's wella, well, soon to be wella." my Father looks her up and down, and smiles, giving his approval of Princess. She has a terrific body. I can't wait until I can shift, so I can really touch that body. Princess looks at him with wonder. My father's hair does not look as if he is over forty years old. His hair is long and black, showing very small hints of silver. My father is very handsome, even at his age of 734.

"Hi," she says, and her voice is the best thing in the world. Who would have thought I could want someone as badly as I want her? I want her in every way.

"I'm King Dramen, Draken's Father."

"Oh, wait, King?" She turns and looks at me. "You're a prince, too? Wow, you just keep all this information to yourself?" I think she is mad, but I see her smile as she turns back to my father, who is still looking at her in awe.

"Umm, hello, King Dramen, right? I'm not good with names, so I'm sorry."

"You said it right, now your name? I've been told it's not Cess, as we thought, so what is your full name?" my father asks. I puff, and purple smoke comes from my mouth and nostrils. I know my Princess doesn't like her name, but she has a beautiful name, and very fitting in this situation.

"Well, you're right, Cess is my nickname and the name I prefer, but my full name is Princess Frances Lamil, sir," she says, fidgeting. I don't like her fidgeting; I let out a growl to get them to back the fuck off her. She made a very big decision to come here.

"What a very fitting name for you, Princess Frances, if you prefer Cess, I will grant you that wish, as you did come and make my son, who is the heir to the throne, change his mind about life. For that, we must prepare a huge celebration for you. I don't think my son likes my asking questions, that growl is for me. So I will let you stay with him. His brothers will move him soon, so he may heal. He is not allowed to shift until he is completely healed, which I suspect will be a few days," my father says, with a smile.

Princess smiles back, and I relax a little. I think they are telling her too much, I don't want her ever to regret coming here.

"Thank you, but you don't have to give me a party. I don't need anything for coming here to stop him from doing something foolish. I am shocked he will be in this state for a couple of days, but that does mean he can't be all demanding and stuff," Princess says, turning and giving me a wink. I growl again, hating that I can't grab her and take her to my room and make sweet love to her until she can't walk. Princess doesn't understand, my father was not giving her an option.

"Cess, when Draken heals, we will celebrate," he says, arching a brow. He is not going to argue with her. "Cess, maybe we should have a talk soon, just you and I, would you be willing?" Fuck! He knows to ask this when I can't talk. I let out a very loud roar, and Princess jumps. I didn't mean to scare her. They need to leave her alone.

"My son is very possessive of you, maybe I will have to allow him in on the conversation."

"I think that will make me more comfortable as well," Princess says. I glance at Showken, who has transformed back into human form right in front of everyone. It's commonly done, but Princess is watching with huge eyes. A servant gives him a wrap for his waist. I wish I could heal faster. Showken comes up to me, smiling.

"Hey, brother, we need to move you out of the stadium so you can get your wounds looked at. I will make sure Cess gets there." I growl and nudge him with my nose. If he thinks Princess is going out of my sight or touch, Showken is asking for trouble when I heal.

"Cess, my brother does not want you to be away from him, not even for a minute."

"Draken, it's okay, I will be right behind you, I promise."

"Cess, you're going to have to get on his back as we carry him out. Draken . . . Draken will kick my ass if you don't, he wants your touch right now."

"You really love your brother, Showken, I would give you a kiss right now, but I remember what happened to Scott, so I will blow you a kiss." Princess blows him a kiss, and I hear all my brothers growl in a laughing way. Princess is so in trouble. Showken reaches up like he has caught it, and puts on a big smile. I let out a fast spit of fire, Showken moves before it can hit him, my brother is testing me.

"Ahh, my brother is gaining strength, Cess, don't do that again. I'm already in trouble because you've seen me naked," Showken says, and Princess blushes. SHIT!

"Okay, if I get on him, umm, I'm scared. I don't know." She turns and looks at me. "Draken, I'm scared to get on you, I mean you're already hurt and, umm, I might fall." Showken tells her she will be fine, I can see the panic in her eyes.

"Cess, you won't fall off when you climb on, in fact, it will make you one with him."

"What?" Princess says, looking more confused. I really need to talk. Nobody can explain it to her.

"Trust me, now we must hurry, I'm sure my brother wants to get started on healing, and my other brothers can't shift, because they have to carry him."

"How many brothers do you have, I mean it seems like a lot."

"There are nine boys altogether, including Draken, and one girl."

"Oh, wow. I guess I don't have a choice. Wait, my family! What do they think has happened to me?"

"They think Draken took you out of town to propose."

I need to figure out how to propose to Princess, the right way.

"You knew I would come?" Cess says to Showken.

"No, my mother said you would come."

My mother only suspected she would come. It was not a certainty, because Princess was so unsure.

"Where is she? I must say thank you." Princess is going to fit right in.

"You will have your chance." Showken comes closer and gets on his knees by my neck, to let Princess climb on my back.

"Showken, you sure I won't fall?" Princess asks. Showken just looks at her.

"Okay, Draken, I'm climbing on you. That sounds dirty," she says, smiling. Yes, it's dirty, Princess, but with you dirty is what I want. She places her foot on Showken's shoulder and begins to pull on my beast to get a good hold. I sigh, for her touch is remarkable. "This is a huge necklace around your neck, Draken. All of the different jewels are beautiful," she says, holding tight. I see my brothers approaching and I feel her tensing up, their size is scaring her.

"I need to pee really bad, I'm going to close my eyes until I'm back on the ground," she says, out loud to anyone listening. My brothers pick me up, moving me to an area for dragons to heal. I'm laid on a purple platform. I see the servants come, waiting for Princess to move as they use a spray on me.

"Cess, they are going to spray Draken with a liquid that will help him heal faster."

"Oh, I guess my face showed my concern. Who are these people, are they dragons too?" Shit, Showken, let me tell her. Layern has changed and comes walking in. Great!

"Showken, Draken would like to tell Cess some things, besides, he is really annoyed right now. He hates that he is in this state," Layern says, standing a few steps away. I hope he doesn't think I'm angry with him.

"No, Draken, I'm fine." I roll my eyes at Showken to reassure him I'm not angry with him at all. "Draken, I'm going to go and make sure Cess has all she needs brought to her immediately," Layern says, leaving the cavern.

As Showken and Princess stand back, Showken hands her a

covering for her entire body. It will protect her from the spray. She's not from this land, so it could harm her if she is not covered.

"What is this for?" she asks.

"Draken will explain more later, but you will be able to see and breathe, but you must put this on before they can spray him," Showken says, gesturing with hands for her to put it on. Princess is always asking questions.

"Okay, I'll put it on," she says, struggling with the covering. One of the servants comes and helps her. "Thank you," she says. They are not allowed to speak unless given permission, so she turns to help with the spray. Once I'm sprayed, the pain starts to go away, and I feel myself getting drowsy. Princess must notice, because she pats me.

"Draken, rest. I won't leave, besides, I'm scared to leave. Your land is very pretty, but I feel like not everyone is happy I'm here. So I won't go wandering around. I want you to rest, I may take a nap myself." I growl in approval. I would know for sure she is safe and not taking a walk. We both sigh and I know she, too, is tired. She snuggles up really close, and I close my eyes to sleep.

***

For the next two days, Princess eats with me and sleeps next to me. My beast is so pleased. She even takes a tour of me, walking around my entire beast, examining everything she can. I love her conversations, and I just listen. "I didn't come planning to stay, but I'm here now, and can't imagine ever being without you." That makes my beast smile and roar. It's pleasing to know she wants to be here.

The time goes by slowly. I finally get the strength to shift back, Princess is asleep. I grab a wrap to cover up, and I pick her up to take her to my bed. She looks so beautiful asleep. I call for fruit and wine to be brought to my room. I need to wash this blood off me. I take a shower and am out fast. I climb into bed and begin planting soft kisses on her neck.

"Draken, you back?" she says, waking up.

"I never was gone, Princess, just in another form," I say, attacking those soft lips and pushing my tongue into her mouth. I need her now. I start removing her shirt, grabbing her breast hard. I want her to be sure it's me, that it's real. I remove her bra, and a moan escapes her mouth. I go back to her mouth, kissing gently.

"Draken, I'm so happy. I love you touching me, please," she whispers.

"I've wanted you, it seems like forever." I pull off her shorts and panties together. Spreading her legs apart, I see the shine of her arousal, all for me.

"How do you want me, Princess, do you want it rough, slow, tell me how you want me and your wish will be granted." I see the blush rising, and I like that sight. She likes that. I whisper more. "I want to lick you all over, not missing a single spot, and Princess, rest assured I won't miss a spot. I want you to climax until you think you can't, and then I'll give you two more. I want to lick your treasure until you scream and beg me to stop. Most of all, I need to have those legs around my waist as I fill you, rocking you into paradise. Would that be fine, Princess?"

"Yes, please." I smile, moving to her feet, and begin with her toes, sucking each one, making sure to bite softly. "Draken, I've missed you."

"I missed you more." I continue my assault on those perfect feet, then long sucks on her calves. I want her to be pleased. I squeeze her thighs as I plant soft kisses, moving closer to her sex, which is radiating heat. Yes, I will take my time with her today, and tonight.

CESS

Oh, Draken is going to have me screaming. I don't know when I got to this room. I assume it's his, as everything is purple and gold, but I can't even look around, Draken is sucking my feet again. "Ohhh, yes, this is amazing." I can't help myself. Draken runs his hands up the inner part of my thighs, placing a thumb inside me as another finger massages my clitoris. I become extremely hot. This feels so good.

"Climax, Princess," he says, and I do. His mouth is at my sex, licking and sucking as I come. As it comes to an end, Draken continues to suck hard. "Yes, Princess, I had to taste you, it's been so long." He leans down, kissing me deeply. I can taste myself on his lips and on his tongue. I feel him entering me, and I yell out in pleasure, "AHHHHHHH!"

"I love you, Princess, you're mine forever." I meet him with each thrust, in . . . out . . . in . . . out. He begins to twist inside me, and it drives me insane. Oh, my . . . he goes deeper inside, stills for a second, and then pulls my legs around his neck, turning his head and biting my legs as he continues to thrust harder, deeper.

"Say it, Cess," he says,

"Draken," I say, panting.

"Louder!"

"DRAKEN!" I yell, louder.

"I love you, Princess," he says, pulling out of me and rolling me onto my stomach. I think he is going to want me on all fours, but no.

"Lie down, remember, Princess, everywhere." He licks my back in long strokes. He holds on to my thighs, giving me small squeezes as he heats me up. My body feels like a flame, yet I like it. I will never get enough of him.

"Draken, oh . . . YESSS!" My thoughts are everywhere right now.

"Give me all of you, Princess," he grabs my hips, moving me close to him, placing kisses on my buttocks and biting gently in between the kisses. Then he devours me from behind with his tongue. He sucks and kisses me in a sensual, sweet way. I feel his hand sliding up my back as he starts a massage. I don't think I can take any more.

"I won't stop loving you, Princess," he says, continuing.

"Ahh, ohh . . . mmmmmm, you, DRAKEN!" He finally comes up, filling me from behind, holding me up. I never knew sex could be this good. I feel like the luckiest woman on the planet.

"Princess, your body is a dream, I love every part of you," he whispers, as I feel the building heat all around us. I feel like I might pass out. He leans over, and I feel his hair on my back as he continues his slow, torturing twists inside me. "Climax again for me, and I will with you." Those words are all I need. I scream and he growls. I feel his hands on my breasts, pinching my nipples. I can't stop it. My body is still going. I scream again and it finally stops, leaving me hot and shaking. He pulls me down on my side as he falls down on the soaked bed. I'm in his embrace, and feel at home.

"Princess, you are my first and only love," he whispers in my ear. Then, he does something I didn't expect. He sings to me. Holy shit! He can sing. His voice is so nice. I don't understand a word he's saying. "For you my Princess, always and only for you."

"Your voice is amazing, Draken, I love you so much it hurts," I say, feeling like I might wake up.

"Thank you for giving me your love, I know I have a lot of explaining to do, but can we just stay like this for a while?" I turn around to see his face. I place my hand on his cheek, and it's so hot.

"Yes, I would love that. I don't want this ever to end," I say, looking into his eyes. After going another couple of rounds, we fall asleep.

***

I hear bath water and feel for Draken, he is not in the bed. I guess I'm still getting baths.

"Draken," I yell for him. He walks out of the bathroom totally nude. I stop breathing. He smiles and his hair is loose and messy, his body is muscle everywhere. I take a long look at his sex, and still can't believe it fits. His legs are so long and strong, every muscle is perfect. He is solid.

"You approve?" he asks, smiling. Oh, his eyes have a slight glow, a purple glow. He can't be real. "What?"

"You are so amazing, and your eyes are glowing," I say. He looks so good.

"Really? I was about to say that yours are glowing, too," he says, smirking. What?

"What? Draken, my eyes don't glow, let me see." I swing my legs over the bed and notice my legs are weak. I can't walk. He strolls over, picking me up and kissing me. I break the kiss. "Draken, I want to see my eyes," I say, and he walks to a huge mirror on the wall. Sure enough, my eyes are not only glowing, they are purple, like his. How did this happen? I look at him, eyes wide in fear. I hope I'm not turning into a dragon. "Draken, my eyes are light purple. I don't have purple eyes. How did it happen?"

"You're mine, Princess, and I also connected with you this time during sex, releasing all of me inside you. You won't turn into a dragon, but you are connected to me. You will fly on my beast without fear now."

"Draken, what else is going to happen?" I ask, looking at my new set of eyes. They look good.

"Your hair will eventually change, but that will be much later. Oh, and you will never die or age now, as long as I'm alive."

"You mean I'm immortal?"

"No, I can die, if you recall. I said you die when I do, not a minute before," he says, kissing me. He pulls my body to his mouth, biting my nipple. I laugh out loud. Draken seems so happy now, happier than I've ever seen him. "Now let's go bathe." He walks us into a room that looks like a magical place. Everything is jeweled. I glance over my shoulder and see a freaking huge bathtub, it's more like a pool. I see flowers floating around and I turn to him.

"I might get used to this." I bite my lip, feeling really amazed.

"I hope you do, Princess, this is just a taste of what I have waiting for you," he says, heading for the pool and taking the stairs down into the water. He is bathing with me. I've never been in the tub with him before, or any man. I shouldn't feel shy, but I do.

"Draken, the water is the right temperature, it's perfect. Thank you for being my prince," I say, smiling. He is a prince for real. He holds on to me, going over to a seat in the water. I look up, and see the sky above us. I smile even harder. This must be a dream.

"I have to hold you, Princess, you can't walk and I don't want you drowning." He turns me and I straddle him.

"Why can't I walk, Draken?" I ask, already knowing the answer. I feel him get hard, and his eyes shine a little brighter. Oh, he is so fine. Damn.

"Why do you stare at me like I'm a treasure?" he asks, pulling me closer.

"Mmmm, umm, Draken, you are more than a treasure, you're a wish come true." He smiles and starts kissing me. We are never going to leave this room if we keep at this. I feel his hands pulling my legs farther apart, and I notice the water is getting warmer.

"Don't be afraid, it will not burn, it's just me, my heat, my beast... Princess, ride me." I feel my body answer his request. I reach for his sex, placing it near mine, and I feel it jumping, shit. I place him inside, making a face as my body adjusts to him.

"Yes Princess, that feels good, I love being inside you, it's my favorite place." I moan as our bodies began to move.

"Hmmm," I begin pushing up and sliding down. I'm not doing this right. I can't think when he feels this good.

"Princess, dance as you're on me." I look at him and began to move to a very slow song that starts playing from somewhere. I twist and grind, getting my rhythm. He joins me, and we never miss a beat, and this becomes more than a bath. It is a continuing from the bed. I get comfortable and really go for it. Draken's head goes back.

"Yes, please, don't stop, Princess."

"I won't." I love this man. We continue with our lovemaking in the bath. I don't even know where the strength comes from, but I'm dancing on him, wanting to give him some of what he gives me. We finally find our release together. Draken takes his time, bathing me with wonderful-smelling cream. I just enjoy the rest of the bath.

***

"Draken, we need to talk," I say, looking in the mirror at the beautiful gown I'm wearing. It's purple, of course, with gold trim. It's very fitted, and has splits all around, showing my legs every time I walk.

"I know. Where do you want to start?"

"How about my father giving me the okay to marry you? I mean, you have not even asked me," I say, smiling. He smiles back. He doesn't have a shirt on, just soft, black, loose-fitting silk pants.

"I know, it's coming. Next?"

"Draken."

"Next, Princess?"

"Okay, my parents think I'm coming to have a wedding at home, but you said I can't ever go back."

"You will have your wedding on earth and here in your new home."

"How? Really? That means I can go back whenever I want?"

"No, Princess, but I will make sure you see your family as much as I can let happen without losing you. This is now your home. Understand?"

"Huh? Draken, what do you mean?"

"Do you have to know everything right now? Your party is starting, and you're the guest of honor," he says, opening the door, and I realize this place is huge. The hall looks like it never ends. I look down and see the purple rug under my feet. It feels soft. I smile, because Draken says, "Shoes are not needed." I walk hand and hand with him towards the music, and I'm getting nervous. I'm about to meet his family, really. This is so scary and exciting. We finally come to a pair of big doors, and Draken turns and looks at me.

"You look beautiful, don't be nervous, I'm here and no one will cross me, trust?" he says, leaning down and giving me a kiss.

"Okay, but don't leave my side. Not once," I say. He pushes the door open and I can't believe my eyes. The room is full of men and women, people are dancing, wearing hardly anything. I glance at Draken and he is smiling. The room is huge, he points ahead and I see a stage of some kind with men standing on it, lots of fine-looking men. They are all staring at me. I look at Draken again, and think maybe staying in the room would have been better. He pulls me through the crowd of people and they make a path for us, bowing as we pass by them. Draken pulls me close, and we finally make it to the stage, where we walk up a huge set of stairs. I don't think I'm going to make it. My legs are still sore. We get to the top and I see Showken eating and smiling, talking with some lady. Gemi is talking with a lady, too, and he is really into a conversation with her, he does stop and give me a smile and nod. I smile back. Layern is sitting watching the crowd. Hawken comes up to us and Draken's smile vanishes.

"Hello, Cess," Hawken says, looking at Draken. "Your eyes are lovely." I blush and lower my head, I hear a growl in my chest and see Draken staring at me. Shit! I guess lowering my head is wrong. Draken is so jealous.

"Hello, Hawken," I reply.

"Draken, the rest of the family is waiting to meet her, are you going to introduce?"

"Yes, I'm on my way to the table," Draken says, turning to me. He plants a soft kiss on my lips, and I feel a heat building. Whoa, not here, too many people.

"Princess, I need to introduce you to the rest of my family, come," he says, pulling me over to a table were all of his family have gathered. The party is still going on, I see all of these beautiful women looking at me strangely, some even frowning. We reach the table and all conversations stop, everyone's eyes are on me. I try to take a couple of steps back, as I feel as if I were on display or something. Draken pulls me forward, wrapping his arm tightly around my waist.

"You're fine," he whispers in my ear. "Princess, you have already met Showken, Layern, Gemi and Hawken, but the one standing, with the red hair, is my brother, Warton. The one next to him with his head shaved on both sides is Brumen. The one who is smiling at you little too much is Fewton. The one with the cocky stare is Domlen. And last but not least, that beautiful lady who is blushing and waving at you is my sister, Beauka. Now, my brothers will introduce themselves one by one, but listen. Beauka is charming and beautiful, which is the meaning of her name, yet she will kill without blinking. Never go anywhere with her alone, never, Princess," Draken says, rubbing my hands.

"Draken, umm, you have a lot of brothers, and you just scared me about your sister. Now I have to . . . oh, here comes a new brother?" I swallow hard and squeeze Draken's hand. I mean, these same people, or dragon thingies, were going to kill him a few days ago. I'm not sure how to act. Oh, two are coming. I have forgotten who they are. They both nod to me and say something to Draken, hugging him. Then all eyes are on me.

"Hello, Cess. I call you that, as we were told that is your preference. I'm soon to be your brother, Fewton," he says. His eyes are a rich milk chocolate. Yikes, he is extremely handsome.

He smiles even more than Showken.

"Fewton, don't make me upset," Draken says, emphasizing the word "upset".

"Draken, I'm just introducing myself to her. So possessive," Fewton says, looking at me. The other is all eyes on me, also. His eyes are a midnight blue, almost black. He finally smiles when I can't take my eyes away.

"Hello," he says, "I'm Domlen, another brother. I already know who you are, Cess. You should not ever fear me, I will never harm you, I'm glad you came and saved my brother. It's nice to meet you and I'll see you around, but I have to collect a gift." Walking past me and Draken. I turn to see where he is going and see a lady waiting for him. She looks amazing. All of these women are beautiful. I look up at Draken as he is talking to Few-something, I don't want to be here at this party. I feel weird, out of place, and everyone is staring at me.

"Draken, he didn't even let me say hello back, I think everyone is looking at me and I don't feel welcome, I want to leave," I say, moving closer to him.

"You feel uncomfortable, unwanted, who has made you feel that way?" he asks, frowning and looking around.

"Draken, it's how everyone is staring and smiling, but not really smiling because they want me here. And the women in this room are all super beautiful, and I'm just . . . "

"You're just the most beautiful woman I've ever seen." He

leans and gives me a kiss. "You are my future wella. You should feel comfortable, and if you don't, you know I can be an ass, as you call me." He gives a wicked grin. He turns towards the crowd, raising both arms, but not letting go of my hands.

"SILENCE!" He waits as it gets quiet. I feel even more on display. I try to push back away. I feel warmth behind me. I turn, and see his mother standing there. She comes and stands on the other side of me, holding my other hand with both of hers. I feel a sense of calm coming over me. She smiles at me, and I can see Showken's grin all the way. The music stops, everyone is now looking at me and Draken. I just want to hide right now, really. I can't believe he did this.

"My Future wella does not feel comfortable," Draken says. "And I don't like that. This party is in her honor, right, Father?"

"Yes, my son." Draken's dad speaks, shit, I should never have told Draken, he overreacts.

"I think that my future wella should be greeted properly, but I sense some resistance. Know that I will take it personally if she continues to have this feeling, someone will be punished," he says, and the silence is scary. Then out of the blue a women yells out.

"I think you have chosen wisely, my Prince. And I wish you happiness. May I present your future wella a gift?" She bows. I'm freaking speechless. I don't want gifts.

"Yes, you may," Draken says. His stare is cold. The woman makes her way up to the front and kneels before us, holding a golden ball.

"I bring this gift to you, future wella to Prince Draken, heir to the throne of Cortamagen. I give you a golden ball for your firstborn," she says. What the hell, I'm not pregnant. These people are crazy. Who gives as a wedding gift a golden ball for a child I don't have?

"That is very generous and thoughtful. You were the first to speak, you are rewarded with coming to the table and sharing a meal with me and my family. Come," he says, gesturing her to the table. She walks up, bowing before his mother, Draken, and me; I don't like this, I really want to leave now. It's not long before the steps are full of all sorts of gifts, jewels, fruit, caged birds, garments, perfumes, oils, flowers, wine and many other things I can't name. Draken turns to me, kissing me. "Your eyes are beautiful, Princess, feel more comfortable?" he says, looking at me.

"No, I can't believe you just threatening everyone if they did not greet me. Draken, they probably hate me more now."

"Princess, this is how it's done. I give a command and it's followed through. I don't care if they approve, but respect will be given. Now let's eat." I just stare in disbelief, turning to see more gifts being presented. This is crazy.

"Cess," Draken's mom calls my name. "My son is right, and if you have a disagreement, never in public. We have much to discuss. The ceremony will be in the next two passing stars. Oh, you don't understand that. How can I say, almost 60 days," she says, urging me to the table and Draken is right on my heel. I can feel his heat. When we make it to the table, suddenly a man yells out. "You disgrace my family, my daughter, Prince Draken Draglen!" he growls. .

DRAKEN

Who the fuck is that? Who calls me out, in my land, in front of my family and my Princess? I see all my brothers stand, and Domlen moving closer to this man. I don't know him, yet he seems familiar.

"Ledo, don't hasten your death," my father says, coming forward. "My son has chosen another, we are grateful for your offer, but we will not be accepting Velca into this family." My father stands like the king he is, I stand next to him, and I see all my brothers are coming forward.

"Your son dishonors you with that HUMAN!" he yells. I growl, and my beast wants out. The people began to scatter, knowing anything could happen.

"You need to leave before-"

"Before what? You kill me, you already have. My daughter will never be with another. She loves him, and you bring another to our land? Death would be easier than to see this kingdom fall into the hands of your son."

"TAKE HIM AWAY NOOOOOOW!" my father commands, making the walls shake, and the people cry out in fear, knowing his wrath can touch many. "THERE ARE WORSE THINGS THAN DEATH AND YOU WILL LEARN THEM!" My father turns and leaves, I'm sure to get control of himself. My mother follows him, as she is the only one who can calm him down. I watch the man yell as he is being taken away. I see Domlen follow. I know he will administer an instant punishment that only he can do. I turn and see my Princess standing by the table, shaking. I go over to her and put my arms around her. If anyone thinks he will scare her and get away with it, he is mistaken.

"You okay, Princess?" I say. She keeps her head down. I place my hand under her chin and lift her head, and see tears. "No, don't cry, Princess. It will be fine, I promise."

"Draken, you had to make the people like me, now a man comes in here yelling about me. I don't belong here, please take me back to your room. I don't want a party," she says, removing her head from my hand and lowering it. I growl loudly. I turn to my brothers who can all see that Princess is crying now. They all come and surround her.

"Cess, you belong here, and we just started the party. Father will be back, if you leave it will only make him feel bad, so please stay and party, dance, okay?" Showken says. Her face is all red from crying. I'm so pissed; this must have to do with the other I was supposed to marry. She steps into my chest.

"I feel like I've stolen you, Draken, I don't want to be a home breaker."

"What? Cess, you're not breaking anything," Hawken says.

"Come dance with me, please?" I say. She looks up at me and I fall even more in love with her. It's her party and she is worrying about someone she doesn't know. I will handle this tomorrow, first thing. I will party tonight. I lead her down the stairs, and a circle is formed for us as we dance.

"Draken," she pleads

"I'm not taking no for an answer, Princess, so get ready to dance for me, now and later," I say, winking. I loved that dance she gave me in the tub. I want another one tonight. She smiles as I start to move, arching a brow at her. I will make my Princess smile, and tomorrow it will be hell for her tears at the party, no one makes her cry. I see her body beginning to move with the beat. I grab her from behind and pull her in to me, placing my hand on her back, and she falls right in, bending and dipping in front of me. My Princess is a very good dancer, that is good, because dancing is such a huge part of my land.

"Draken, you know music is my weakness, but thank you for

dancing with me now, and later," she says, making me want to take her now. Her eyes are beautiful, and they say she's mine. My brothers take the floor, taking partners and the floor fills up as we dance. I see my parents come back, and my mother smiles at me. I know she has calmed him. When my father is angry, lots of innocents can die. I dance, taking Princess with me as she turns into me, grinding, sliding her hands down my body, lifting her leg and wrapping it around me as I dip her. I love seeing her like this, dancing is her element. It always calms and relaxes her.

"I can't wait for you to dance later, with no clothes," I say in her ear whispering. She closes her eyes, feeling the music. We dance for another two songs before she is finally laughing and having fun. My brothers make sure to dance as sexily as possible. Especially Layern, he is the best dancer. I look for my sister; she is sitting watching me and Princess. I hope she is not going to give Princess a hard time. She has been the only girl in the royal family for a while. I turn my attention to Princess as she is having a good time. I hear the applause, as she shows off her moves. I also see the men smiling, wishing they could have her, well not even in their dreams. She's all mine.

"You hungry?" I ask. She shakes her head no.

"I want to dance longer, you can really dance, for being an ass," she says, laughing. This is how I want her, happy, not tearful.

"Dancing is a part of us, we all dance, but I'm sure you see Layern's dancing skills exceed all of ours, and I see you keep up with him very well, Princess."

"Yes, I see Layern is good, but I may not be able to keep up with him, as he more than likely can dance all night."

"I can do things all night besides dancing, would you like to see?"

"Hmmm, Draken. Are you trying to get me away so you can have your way with me?" She smiles, and I feel so good with her in my arms. I love the touch of her soft skin, her smell is intoxicating and her love sustains me. I'll do anything for her, even get her home to have a wedding with her family and then do one here. She deserves two weddings.

"Yes, I want to take you from this room and make love to you, can we go?"

"We haven't eaten yet," she says, giggling.

"Oh, you want to eat now? Okay, I will have food waiting in the room, come," I say. I glance at Showken, and he nods and looks at a servant, making sure food will be delivered before we arrive. I nod to my brother. I start dancing out of the door with Princess, I see my mother blow me a kiss and my dad give me a nod.

"Draken, you made me feel so much better, I love dancing, and you knew what to do. Thank you." She places her hands on my face and gives me a kiss. I'm going to ravish her in the room. We begin our walk there. I escort her through the garden. The flowers are swaying with the music. I smile because Princess' expression is priceless.

"Draken, when you say everyone dances, does that include flowers? I've never seen anything like this. It's so magical here, I see why you love this place," she says as she moves back and forth.

"It's magical with you, and I would have given it all up for you, because you are my magic, my smile and without that I would be lost. I can't believe I even considered anything else with you, I was a fool, but not any more. I'll never stop loving you, and I hope you will grant me the privilege of having your love," I say, knowing my words are true. She came here for me, and she will always come first.

"Draken, if I ever doubted your love, your willingness to die, though foolish, pushed away any questions I had. I love you, too, and I'm hungry now."

"Okay, I will get you there quicker, close your eyes."

"Why?"

"Please, Princess. You and all these questions," I say, waiting for her eyes to close. When she does, I immediately teleport us to my room, using one of my powers.

"Wow, how many powers do you have?" she asks. I smile and walk around her slowly, taking in her body.

"I have a few, nothing that can't be discussed later, Princess. I would rather show you other things, okay?'

"I - okay." I walk her to my balcony, and there awaits a table of choice meat, fruit, vegetables and desserts.

"Draken, that outburst at the party was about, your, umm, other bride-to-be," she says, choosing a handful of grapes. I walk over and pull out her chair. I need to explain some things to her.

"Princess, yes, the outburst was about that, but I've never met her. In my land, usually the wella, or bride, is chosen only for the one heir to the throne. The reason is to ensure the legacy continues. Then I met you and fell in love. I had no idea that if an heir falls in love with a human the possibility is that she is a Key. A Key is what keeps the portal open, from here to earth. I know you don't understand all of this, but if you just trust me, I will explain more every day until you get it, okay?" I say, hoping she kind of gets it. I'm not sure. I still have to do an official proposal, so I will get started on that once she's asleep.

"I don't understand, but I'll trust you, do you think the other woman is really pissed?"

"Oh, I'm sure she's not happy, but she'll have to live with it, because you are my Princess forever." I lean in for a kiss.

"Oh, Draken, we need to go back home to plan my wedding there, I need my father to walk me down the aisle. Besides, D has to be there for me. I need to know, will all your brothers and parents be at the wedding?"

"Of course, they can travel just fine. I will have it set up that we go back in a few days, good?"

"Good. Now, I'm going to get me a piece of this strawberry

cake," she says, diving right in for dessert first. The night consists of food, making love, talking and more lovemaking. When we finally fall asleep, I make a mental note to prepare her proposal for tomorrow. I smile to myself, as I have an idea in my head for my Princess.

CESS

Last night was great. My ex-fiancé's ex-soon-to-be-father-in-law crashed the party, and his outburst interrupted the celebration, but once it was under control I had fun. I can lie in this bed all morning. Wait, Draken is not in here. Where is he? I sit up, and really get a look at the room. The bed is huge, no dressers in the room, but a seating area and an entire wall of books. This is definitely a man's room; I do like the purple and gold color scheme. I need to take a bath, but I'm sure walking is going to be a problem again, Draken did not let up last night. I hear the door open, and he walks in, all smiles. I can't help but feel butterflies when I see him.

"Princess, your bath is waiting for you; I heard you wake, and came to carry you."

"So, are you always going to carry me to take a bath, and will I ever be able to stand and take a shower?" I smile as he pulls the covers back and his eyes roam my body. "Draken, focus. Did you hear a word I just said?"

"Yes, you will be able to stand to take a shower, one day. There is a waterfall for you if you like." He gives me a smile, but I think he is withholding information.

"Draken, what are you hiding?"

"Nothing, come," he says, lifting me out of bed. He walks me into the bathroom and lowers me into the purple stone tub. He makes sure I'm on a seat. The water is amazing, and without notice a waterfall begins to flow right from the ceiling, it's so relaxing and comforting.

"Oh, Draken, this feels amazing. I may never leave," I say, letting the water fall over my face. I lean back and the water is now hitting my chest. It's perfect, I have never seen this before, but I am in a magical place. I grin to myself.

"Princess, you will be able to walk when you are finished with your bath; there is a dress that will be waiting for you."

"Draken, whose clothes are these?" I know he doesn't have women's clothes on hand.

"Oh, my mother and sister went shopping for you," he grins, and walks away. I'm just looking at the doorway with my mouth open, why are his mother and sister going shopping for me, and where the heck is the mall in this place. Draken has not told me everything, I'm sure. I take my time and have a wonderful bath.

When I finally get out of the water, my body feels really good, and although my legs are sore, my smile is big. I feel so great, wrapping the towel around me I walk into the room and there is a golden gown lying on a made bed. When did the bed get made? Shit, I have to keep my ears open. I go over and touch the gown, and it's silk. Wow, this is really pretty, the bodice has all of this… no freaking way! Are those diamonds? Can't be! I keep looking and yes, I've seen plenty of diamonds, and this dress is gold with diamonds across the bodice. Damn, I thought we had money. I notice there are no shoes. What is it with no shoes here? I see some perfume on the bed and spray myself with it. I brush my hair. I wish makeup was on the bed, too. I sit on the bed and wait for Draken. I hope he's not long. Right away, I hear his growl in my ears like a call. I get up and walk slowly to the door. I'm not sure if I should leave without him, what if I get lost? The growl in my chest is more intense now. Shit, he must want me to come out. I stand at the door, hesitating to come out. What the hell, I'm in another realm, I might as well explore. I open the door and see Showken, Gemi, Layern, Brumen, Domlen, Hawken, Fewton, and Warton all standing up against the wall, looking like models. None of them has on a shirt, and they are all wearing pants, with no shoes. That's when I notice they all have the same tattoo on their chests, across the heart. How did I remember all their names, I'm not sure, but they all look amazing.

"What are you all doing?" I ask, not taking one step out of the room.

"Cess, we are here to escort you," Showken says, giving a huge grin.

"Why does it take all of you? Where's Draken?"

"Getting pissed, because you are not on your way, let's go, please," Layern says. I step out of the room. I stand on that soft rug and smile. I start getting grins back from the brothers, and then I feel the growl in my chest.

"Okay, he's getting annoyed, I'm ready. Should I, what do I do?"

"Oh, we are not touching you, Cess, follow us," Showken says, as he turns and begins to walk, with the brothers walking two at a time behind him. I walk behind the last pair, Layern and Domlen. "I'm nervous, you guys," I say.

"I know," Layern says, turning his head a little and giving me a smile. The others keep looking forward. When we go down some stairs and down another hall, the floor is warm and feels good on my feet, like a massage. We finally come to double doors, and Showken pushes them open. We walk into a huge, beautiful garden. Everything is colorful. There are people around, all dressed in gowns and things, but I don't see Draken. I do see his mother and sister and even his dad. They are wearing crowns; I look at his brothers and notice they, too, have on crowns, why didn't I notice that before? Everyone looks so happy. What is going on? I don't understand. This can't be my wedding; I want to choose some things myself. His brothers start to separate, and I find that I'm in the middle of everyone. I'm feeling all weird inside. I turn and see Draken coming towards me in loose purple slacks, like silk pajamas. My mouth falls open. He takes his time coming towards me, stopping about five feet away. What's going on, I don't have a clue. When I see him starting to kneel down, my heart starts to beat fast. Holy shit, he's proposing like this. His hair is hanging loose, but looks very nice, and he smiles at me. Then he speaks.

"Princess Francis Lamil, would you accept the responsibility of moving forward to become my wella, forever?" he says, and mouths "I love you" to me. I feel the tears running down my face and start nodding yes, but I hear Showken say:

"Cess, say it out loud."

"Yes, I will become your whatever, Draken." I can't stop my feet from moving, and I run right to him, kneeling with him, and we kiss very passionately. I hear the growls of his brothers, and people clapping. Then a crowd of kids dances around us, making all these weird noises. I know this must be part of the ceremony. I can't wait to have him in my arms.

"You know, there is more to this, but it's my proposal, so who cares," Draken says, wiping away my tears with his fingers. "I love you, Princess and now you are officially engaged."

"Yes, I am." I smile.

"Would you like your ring?" Oh, I totally forgot about a ring.

"Yes, I would."

He nods to Showken, who comes over and hands him a box. It's too big to be a ring box, right? He opens it, and my eyes nearly pop out of my head. The ring is in the shape of a dragon, and I don't know what jewel this is, but he picks it up and slides it onto my left hand. It starts to reshape on my hand before my eyes, as the dragon encloses its body with its wings, and now it looks like a smooth stone. I have a dragon on my finger. Draken is holding a gold and diamond ring that looks like it's about 8 or 9 carats. It's cut in the shape of a heart.

"Oh, Draken, it's beautiful, I love it!" I lean in and kiss him, again. Not too long, the kids are still dancing. "Draken, why two rings?" I ask, admiring the ring on my finger. I can't believe it moves and it's a dragon, and it's purple.

"The second ring is for when we go to earth. This ring will get fussy if not in our land," he says, smiling.

"What a way to propose! I love it, Draken, but I was already willing, you didn't have to do all this."

"Yes, I did." He grins. "You don't understand, do you? When I marry, Princess, I take over the throne and run the land; you'll be queen, but my Princess forever." He stands, lifting me up with him. I love to see the children dance. I smile, and then we turn and everyone is nodding and clapping and I feel like a real princess in a fairy tale. We move over to a seating area as people line up to congratulate us. Everyone looks happy, and I don't like all this attention, but with Draken beside me I can deal with it. I see Showken and his other brothers eating everything up.

"Draken, who are all these people?" I ask.

"These are my family, uncles, cousins, my family," he says, making sure to nod when approached.

"You have a huge family," I say, thinking wow, I hope they all don't come to Earth. We will need to rent a stadium.

"Draken, when did you plan this?"

"This morning, while you slept."

"You are so sneaky, but I love you," I say, giving him a kiss on the cheek. The way this looks, with the people dancing and greeting us, you would think this was the wedding.

"Draken, how big will the wedding be?"

"Everyone will come, Princess, and I do mean everyone."

What kind of answer is that? We sit as people come and go, When his brothers are standing in front of us, I'm handed a glass of wine. Then they speak, all together.

"In this time of celebration, we, the Draglen brothers, promise to protect your future wella until you are joined as one." They look at me. "We promise to watch over you and protect you until you are one with our heir, Prince Draken Draglen. Do you accept our help, Princess Francis Lamil?" Why is everything so formal?

"Yes," I say, hoping that is all I have to do. Draken looks at me.

"Princess, I will fly with my brothers now, to celebrate, but one will stay with you, whom do you choose?" I wonder whether he is going to change right now, will I see it?

"Oh, umm, well," I see Showken smiling. "I choose Showken, then," I say, and Showken comes and stands next to Draken.

"Okay, Princess, Showken will stay, but I can be here very fast. Now, I will go and change into beast, will you watch?" I nod and smile. I have to pee all of a sudden. If I have got this right, they are all going to change into dragons right now. Shit, I have got to pee. I know Draken would not hurt me, but what about the others?

"Yes, I will watch." I say, in a high pitched voice.

"Princess, you don't have to," he says, but I see the disappointment in his eyes.

"No, I'm fine. I want to see, I mean, you will be my husband soon," I say, smiling. He gets up and walks toward the open field with his brothers; I see them playing around, pushing each other and laughing. They look so happy. It must be great to fly.

"Draken is going to try and show off," Showken says, looking at me. "I can outfly him any day," he says, smirking.

"Behave, Showken. You are so easy to love."

"Yes, I am. I'm glad he has you, Cess, and I'm glad to have you in the family," Showken says, and I see the serious side. I smile.

"I'm glad I'm with him, too." I see that he will change first.

He looks like he is enjoying this. "Showken, does it hurt to change, or feel good?"

"Ohh, it feels really good to change into beast."

"Okay." I really need to pee, my man is going to change right in front of me. I'm scared. I hope I don't pass out. I see his body stretching and growing, and it's like his skin is breaking. I really need to pee now. I can see the purple. Oh his wings are huge. I continue to watch, and his hand rips and claws come forth. He shakes, and before I know it he is a dragon, spitting fire, growling, the whole nine yards. Shit!

"It's awesome, right?"

"Yep." I can't say anything but wow right now. I'm marrying a dragon for real, not a fake dragon. He looks at me and I feel the growl in my chest, and heat that shoots right in between my legs. Damn that felt good. He nods and takes off into the sky. His brothers follow behind him, one after the other, until the sky is filled with dragons, who look like they are playing. This can't be real.

"So, Cess, what do you think?" he says, happily.

"I, umm . . . it was awesome. Yes, awesome," I say, watching them in the sky. I see Draken twirling and shooting up really fast, and also blowing smoke out of his nostrils.

"They will be gone for at least an hour, let's eat," he says. I can't eat, it will surely come up. I can deal with seeing the dragon, but changing is like, I don't know, I just prefer not to see that part.

"Sure, we can eat." Showken calls for food, and pretty soon we have everything in front of us. I pick up a pear and take a bite. I start thinking about our wedding on earth, and how I have to deal with two weddings. I would prefer only one, but I'm sure Draken wants a wedding here, in his land. He said everyone would come, I'm not sure what that means, but this is a large amount of people out in their garden. I can only imagine the wedding. I look at my ring and smile; it's so unique and beautiful, I love it.

"It can never be removed unless Draken takes it off," Showken says, watching me looking at my ring.

"I will never take it off," I say, looking at him.

"That ring will protect you, Cess. Also, it's special, and was made for you especially."

"How is that possible, Draken says he just got this together," I say, frowning. Showken is not making sense.

"Trust me, it was made a long time ago. Someone must have known you would come," Showken says, continuing to eat everything near him on the table. I watch in wonder as Draken plays in the sky. How often will he need to fly, and will I ever go with him? Do I want to? Yes, I just have to lay down the rules on spinning, flipping and spitting fire. I will have children with him, oh God, what will they be? Will I bear a dragon or human, I . . . whoa, I feel a growl in my chest, and heat again. I hold on to the chair with both hands as I feel the need of him again.

"Oh, he can sense you Cess, and your questions are many." He chuckles. I think privacy does not exist in this family, or world, more than likely. "Yes, your arousal is sensed as well." Shit, I need to learn how to control that.

"Thanks for letting me know that, Showken," I say, rolling my eyes. I sip from my glass of wine, and continue to look at the people all around.

"Any time, Cess," he says, smiling.

"I think you need a woman, Showken," I say.

"Really? Well, Cess, I'll have you know I have women all the time, but if you're referring to getting married like Draken, I like dating. I'll always be single," he says, and instead of smiling he has a strange look on his face. I wonder if he really does mean that? I'll ask Draken later. Oh, he's flying down, I can't wait till he is back by my side. I put my glass down as he comes and lands, so smooth. He looks so powerful. I can't wait to get him back to the room. His sending me heat like that has me feeling all kinds of feelings. I stand to watch as he begins to change back. It's a lot faster when he changes back into human form. I watch in amazement this time. He is greeted with a wrap, and starts straight for me. I smile, wanting him back. He finally reaches me.

"Princess, are you ready to go take a tour of our castle?" Draken asks.

DRAKEN

I'm so happy right now. I have my Princess with me and I'm taking her on a tour of the castle. Her new home.

"Draken, it's so big and beautiful. Do you all stay in the castle?" she asks.

"Yes, the castle is our home; none of us would ever leave. It's your home, too," I say, pulling her into one of the many rooms. I need to touch and kiss that soft skin, pushing her up against the wall will allow this.

"Draken, what are you doing? What if someone comes in?" she asks. What she doesn't know is that this section is ours, for when we start to have children.

"No one will come in, now I need a taste," I say, dropping to my knees. Her face reddens quickly. I like to keep her on her toes.

"Draken, right now?"

"Mmmmm, yes, Princess," I reply, placing my hands on her ankles, moving in between her legs, I grab each leg, making sure her thighs are on my shoulders. She slides down the door as I hold her backside, and her treasure is all my pleasure. She must have wondered why panties are never going to be laid out for her. I like to take her without fussing with panties. I feel her hands on my shoulders, as she squeezes I growl. I love pleasuring my Princess.

"Draken, I . . . ohhh . . . I-"

"Say it."

"Draaa-"

"Say it," I command.

"Draken," she whispers, which makes a very loud growl exit my mouth. She knows I like her to scream, she's scared of being caught.

"Louder!"

"Draken, please. Someone may hear us, what if . . . ahhh. I-"

"LOUDER!"

"DRAKEEEEEN!" she yells as she climaxes. I hold her there as she comes down and her shaking stops. Placing her feet on the floor and keeping her steady, I rise and share her treasure with her, giving a long, deep kiss and enjoying her moans. She has finally found her voice.

"Draken," she says, panting slowly. "That, I want to pleasure you, too."

"Okay, but come, we have to go see my sister. She has been asking why you are not coming around. Don't worry, I see the frown on your face. I reminded her of how she can sometimes not be a nice dragon," I say, arching a brow.

"Well, I don't want to go if she is going to be, I don't know, weird or scary."

"She will never do that in front of me. Beauka has been hurt and holds a lot of pain, but I think when she finds a love, then it could be safe for you to be alone with her. Until then, never," I say, hoping that she is reassured, besides, I have given her great protection in her ring.

"Well, I guess let's go see your sister," she says, making a weird face. I love how her emotions just come out. When we come to Beauka's section, she is in the hall, looking beautiful as usual. Beauka has the same color hair as I do, but with blue-green eyes. She is very smart, intense and dangerous when she wants to be.

"Hello, my brother, I'm so glad you are joining me for some tea," she says. Princess looks hesitant. Maybe I told her too much, but I will always tell Princess the truth.

"Hello, my dear sister," I turn, pulling Princess closer. "You have met Princess already."

"Yes, I will call her by what comforts her. Hello, Cess, I'm glad you are here for tea. I'm sure Draken has told you lies about me, but I assure you I'm the calmest person among everyone in this castle. Come, let's have some tea and dessert. I love desserts," Beauka says, turning and waving us into her living space. Beauka has a huge living space, she has been the only girl for years, so she might be friendly, yet my sister can be jealous. We sit and she pours the tea, not taking her eyes off Princess. I growl, and she nods her understanding that she is not exempt when it comes to Princess.

"So, Cess, how are you adjusting to our land?" she asks.

"Well, it's very pretty and magical. I love everything about this place," Princess says. I smile, hoping that they will be good friends, Cess will need female companionship

"Yes, it is. So, is my brother good to you?"

"Oh yes," she blushes. "He is such a dream to me, I love him very much." That makes me smile. Beauka makes us each a plate of cakes, and fills our cups with tea. I don't like tea, but to make my sister smile I will drink it.

"Thank you, sis, it looks amazing. Did you help decide on what desserts?" I ask, making conversation. I love my sister, but she and I don't always see eye to eye, especially when we fly. That is why I avoid flying with Beauka. Domlen can handle her so much better.

"Yes, Draken, you know I make all decisions about myself," she smiles at Princess. "Do you plan to give Draken heirs?"

"Oh, well we haven't discussed children yet," Princess says, lifting her cup and taking a drink. I should have warned her about

Beauka's tea. She usually puts in her own specialty. It will make you drowsy if you're not used to it. I notice Princess' eyes are getting droopy. I think it's time to take her to bed.

"Well, sister, Princess is getting tired. I've showed her tons of the castle, so I think we will be going," I say, realizing Princess needs to rest.

"Of course, brother, take care, Cess, and maybe we could spend some girl time together," Beauka says, with a huge smile. We leave Beauka's living space. When we are in the hall, I hold Princess in my arms and, closing my eyes, I take us instantly to my room. I don't like instant transport, as it can make us weak as dragons. I lay her on the bed and she falls into a deep sleep. I watch her as she sleeps peacefully. Beauka's tea will not do any harm, it just puts you to sleep. That is what she likes. I call for Showken, and he arrives outside the hall.

"Showken, Princess is sleeping," I say, arching a brow. "We had tea with Beauka,"

"I don't have tea with our sister, she is really crazy. So, what do you need, Draken?" Showken says, shuddering just thinking about Beauka's tea.

"I need to talk with Velca. I need to apologize for having her life waste away. I don't want her to feel she wasn't good enough. I just want her to understand Princess is my love. So, I need you to arrange a meeting with her and her mother, as her father is in holding. He crossed me with Princess, but I would like to speak with his wife and daughter, with Princess present, of course. Can you arrange?"

"Yeah, sure. Although you owe nothing to anyone. She is still going to be pissed, but I see why you are sending me, as I can help convince her with my charm," Showken says, winking.

"Showken, don't seduce her. I just want a meeting."

"Okay, Draken. I want to ask you something."

I study Showken for a second. Then I see he looks serious.

"I want to know are you worried about getting bored with Cess, I mean you love her, but we are talking forever. Plus, you have not said anything about taking on a Giver. Which is common knowledge and is accepted," Showken says. I control my beast from growling at him.

"I don't want anyone but Princess, you don't understand because you have never loved. When you do, I will remember this conversation, brother, at your wedding. Now, go . . . " I pause, smelling an unfamiliar scent in the castle.

"Do you smell that?" I take a long breath and I'm sure someone is in the house that should not be.

"Yes, I do smell that, it's another dragon for sure, maybe a few more," Showken says, as his beast comes forth. Something is not right.

"I need to go to Princess." I turn and open the door, and see a woman with long, light-purple hair. I growl, and she changes right before my eyes into another dragon. FUUUUUCCCKK! I growl,

Showken standing, glaring. Hawken and Layern rush in the room soon after.

"Draken, Velca's mother and her brothers were on the grounds. I didn't get a fix on them, because Velca's mother has your smell for some reason. I did, however, feel an enormous amount of anger towards Cess. I'm sorry, Draken, they are no longer in Cortamagen, but are in Meltawen. You know we don't really get along with the family that rules that land, so if we go, it will mean war." I try to focus on what Layern says, but I feel Princess' fear. I will find her.

"Layern, war it is. I want Princess back tonight, and if the entire land goes up in flames, so be it." How could I not protect her? "KILL EVERYONE!" I yell. I hope Princess learns quickly about her ring.

"Draken, they will all die, we promised to protect Cess, and we have failed. Forgive us, brother." I see the hurt in my brothers eyes. Everyone's beast is going to be released. Beauka comes in, spitting fire.

"Who dares come to our home and steal my new sister? I fly with you tonight." Beauka turns and walks out. "LETS GOOO!" she yells. I close my eyes and we are in the garden where I proposed, I transform along with my brothers, and for the first time, Beauka. GRRRRRR, who has touched MY Princess. You will die! I'm coming to get you, Princess, hold on.

CESS

What the hell is going on? I remember tea with Beauka and Draken, yes, Draken hugged me. I went to sleep. A woman is standing over me, speaking another language, but I can tell she is angry. I slowly open my eyes, and see another pair of eyes staring fiercely at me. I become immediately scared and now I have to pee, really badly.

"Umm, who are you, and where's Draken?" I ask, scared of the response, please Draken, if you can hear me, I'm scared.

"You are the little human who stole my daughter's right. She was supposed to be queen one day, now my husband will die, my daughter is broken and you think you will get a happy ending? It won't happen, human. I hate humans, and it will be a pleasure to kill you," she snarls. She nods to a man who is standing next to her, and he opens the gate of the prison where she's holding me captive.

"Wait, you're going to kill me, I had no idea Draken was supposed to marry your daughter, but if she wants him I will back out," I say, swallowing and hoping she will take my deal. She grasps the man's arm and they walk towards me.

"You stupid little human, he will never let you go, he marked you. You have his eye color. He was going to die for you and I hoped he would, but you showed up and caused us more embarrassment. I want you on display, for even though I know he will kill me, he will want death, too, after you perish." Her eyes take on a glow that makes me want to pee right there. The man comes and grabs my arm, squeezing tightly. That is when I hear the growl.

"You should not be touching me, I think it's going to get bad for you," I say, looking at the man. He grins and I see fangs. What is he?

"You bring her," the woman says to the man, who grasps my hands together in one of his, and drags me behind her.

"Please, let me go. I don't know anything about this. I will go home. I promise she can have him."

"Quiet," she growls. The man drags me to the center of a room where a group of angry people has gathered. Please, Draken, hurry, I don't want to die. I hear the growling, and it's getting louder and more intense. Then I hear Draken's voice in my head, "Princess, use your ring." Use the ring? Get your ass here, Draken, this is a ring not a . . . the ring did move from a dragon, covering its body. I don't know how to use the fucking ring. All these people around me are speaking in that language, yelling at me. All of this because he decided not to marry her daughter, then a woman with long black hair comes running over to me.

"What have you done, mother?" she says, concern in her eyes. This woman is beautiful. Then I remember. She just called the one who says she is going to kill me "Mother". This is supposed to be Draken's wife. I'm not nearly as beautiful as she is.

"I'm defending you, Velca. That human you are looking at sleeps with Draken, and will be queen. It was your birthright, and she comes and steals it."

"You shouldn't have done this! Prince Draken is going to kill us all! You sentenced us all to death!" She turns and looks at me. "I'm sorry, I do not hate you. I had nothing to do with this. Do you believe me?" I say nothing, still mesmerized by her beauty.

"I believe you. Tell your mother this is not the way, I will let you have him," I say, whispering very low.

"Human, I can still hear you, and nothing will stop me. Velca, do you know your father is being held? You want me to let her go? Even knowing it's her fault?"

"Yes," Velca says, hurt. "Father should not have gone, none of you. My brothers will die because of your coldness, this-" Velca closes her eyes and takes a deep breath. "Prince Draken made his choice, I respect it, I may be hurt, but I do not believe in violence. I want her released now. He's coming, Mother, and he will destroy everyone, including me. Is that what you want? Release her, and maybe we can save the land that you sealed with death, already."

I feel a burning inside me, I hear his voice again. "Princess, use the ring, speak to it." I raise my hand to my mouth and say, "Help," to the ring. Nothing happens. I can hear Velca and her mother facing off. The people start yelling at me again, and tears start to roll down my cheeks. I'm so scared. Tears begin to drip onto my ring, and I feel it shifting on my finger. The dragon on my ring begins to expand and I want to run, but the wings grow and start shielding my body. I hear Velca's mother scream, and she shoots fire at me, but I'm completely covered now. I can see out, and the flames she shoots are bouncing off. Thank God. Please hurry, Draken, this woman is trying to burn me alive. I hear the growl and it's close, really close. That's when I start hearing screams and cries. I look up and see a dragon hand ripping the roof off. It's purple, it's Draken, yes!

Velca falls to the ground. I see a green and greenish-blue dragon flying overhead. Draken is burning everything he sees, and the others are turning into dragons as he fights. Oh God, he leans his head in and rips apart the man who dragged me. I feel something warm going down my legs, shit, I've peed on myself. I've just seen Draken rip someone into pieces. Draken reaches for

Velca, and I start yelling.

"Nooo, Draken! Don't, she is innocent, please noooo!" I yell, trying to get his attention. He turns and looks at me, growling, and fire comes out of his mouth, blowing over me. It blows out the wall behind me, and people are on fire. He's burning them before they can change. I don't want Velca dead, she tried to help me, and the least I can do is try to save her, too. Her mother has changed into a dragon and is flying into the air, I suppose to fight. Draken sets Velca down. She runs over to me.

"Can you hear me?" I ask.

"Yes," she says, crying. "Thank you, thank you for saving me." We both look up as the green and the other greenish-blue dragon rip Velca's mother apart, burning her in the air. I look at Velca, who has tears and pain in her eyes. I feel bad for her. She lost the man she was supposed to marry, and now both her parents are gone. Draken walks in. He must have changed back to human form. He walks right up to Velca and pulls her to her feet, looking stern.

"Why does Princess feel you should be spared?" Draken asks. I see her arm is blistering from a burn.

"I . . . Prince Draken, I promise." She winces from the pain. His nails are digging into her flesh. "I didn't know until my servant came and said my mother had done a terrible thing. I would never be a part of this." He glares, walks over to me and waves his hand, and the wings begin to get smaller. They finally goes back into place and my ring is my ring again.

"Draken, I was so scared," I say, curling into his chest for protection. "She's telling you the truth, Draken, she didn't know, she tried to help me." He stares at her and turns his head as Layern, Gemi and Domlen walk in with four men.

"These are your brothers?" He turns to Velca and asks. His face is cold, his eyes bright and glaring. Shit, he looks scary.

"They came to my castle to help your mother, right?"

"Yes, Prince Draken," she says.

"Then they will die tonight." He sets one on fire instantly. I scream, and darkness finds me.

***

"Draken, Draken." I'm back in bed, and he is wrapped around me. Oh, thank God, it was a dream, a terrible nightmare. I begin to touch his face gently as he sleeps. Finding my hands exploring his face, lips, chin, rubbing his facial hair, I love him so much. I lean over to kiss him, and he flips me onto my back and smiles.

"Good morning, Princess. I see you are doing much better. I'm so happy you are, I thought you would never stop screaming." He leans down and starts planting kisses on my neck and cheeks.

"Screaming?" What is he talking about? Could I have been screaming in my nightmare?

"Princess, stop frowning. You know when you'd seen my

dragon in full rage you were pretty scared," he says, kissing me. I can't move. It was real. The kidnapping, the dragons fighting, it wasn't a dream?

"Draken, umm, I thought it was a dream. I . . . I, that really happened, all of it?"

He says, tilting his head, "Are you frightened of me?"

"Draken, that is not . . . I was frightened. I'm not sure if I was frightened of you," I say, looking down.

"You are in bed with me, your breasts are on my chest, your legs around my waist." He looks down and smells me. "You smell of need for me," he says, annoyed. "Never be afraid of the one you want, love, Princess. I killed last night, and will do it again if anyone dares to try to harm you. I'm a dragon first and a man second. The beast in me will always protect you, and we will both love you." He is still holding his body over me, waiting for my response. I love him and his dragon. He came for me and made sure I was safe. I lift my hands and pull his shoulders towards me.

"I'm sorry, Draken, I love you and your dragon, I was just scared. I've never seen anything like that, but I know what you are, and I called for you because I knew you would come. I'm sorry if I seem, umm, ungrateful. Will you make love to me now? I need your touch. Oh, wait! I peed on myself, I need to shower," I say, trying to come out of his hold.

"I bathed you, Princess, you are mine, I knew what happened when it happened. I cleaned you when we came home. I must say,

I would like to do that again, but when you are fully awake." He smiles and leans down, pushing his tongue into my mouth, rocking his body over me, teasing me with his sex over mine. I feel it slide up and down me. My body needs him now.

"Princess, you want it, you grab it and place it inside you, for I'm yours, too," he says, licking his lips. I find myself warm all over. I reach out and grab his sex and give it a good squeeze that causes him to moan out loud. I place it right at my entrance, and my body jumps toward him.

"Push me in, Princess, I love your hands on me," he says. "It's the best feeling ever, your hands on me." Those words make my body respond. I slide him in and feel my body stretching to accept him. I moan. "Ohhhhh."

"I love you, Princess, I'll always protect you, now enjoy," he says, and I'm lost in him, going places with my body that I didn't know existed. He's reminding me how important I am to him, and how he will always kill for me, forever. I rub my hands down his strong back and enjoy, like he said.

***

We eat a tray of cheese, fruit and wine. He gives me butterflies just looking at him. Will I ever get over this feeling? I hope not, but I need to say thank you to the others.

"Draken, I have to say thank you to the others. You even said during our bath today that Beauka came, the one you said is dangerous, she came for me, too. I have to say thank you. Can you arrange that, please?" I ask. He looks at me lustfully.

"Yes, I can arrange that. I just want to say, you are truly one of a kind. I do need to know what you want me to do with Velca. You saved her and didn't tell me what to do." Oh, his other ex-soon-to-be-wife.

"I don' t know. Let her live, of course. She saved my life, and she deserves to live and find love one day. I hope. I'm not ready to become BFF's with her, but can you make sure she has a place to live?" I ask. He fills his mouth with fruit and cheese. I just stare at how, even like this, he looks sexy as hell.

"Okay, Princess, anything for you. I will make sure you get your chance to speak to your family," he says, smiling. "Let's get dressed. If you open the door on your side of the bed, I had a closet put in for you, I should say Beauka requested you have one. She and my mother stocked it for you already." He climbs out of bed and goes to a hidden wall. He touches it and it opens, revealing a cupboard.

"Princess, go dress, before I come and attack you again." I smile and go to the purple and gold door. I open it slowly, not knowing what to expect. I see dresses and a wall of jewels, bracelets, necklaces, no pants or shorts or t-shirts. I'm going to have to talk with Draken about this. There are no shoes, either. Draken comes up behind me, wrapping his arms around me.

"I like you in dresses, besides, they have benefits, now hurry. I have already sent word that everyone is to gather in the family hall," he says, pulling away. I walk in, pull out the first dress I see and put it on. It has a built-in bra. Laughing to myself, I think Draken is going to attack me all the time. I walk out and we head to the family space he is talking about. This place is huge. We are silent as we walk, and I embrace that silence. I have a chance really to enjoy the sights. The windows are huge, some with glass, some without. Everything is elegant and beautiful. Jewels are on everything. We finally make it to the family space, I think that's the name. I see everyone in there, they are laughing, and eating, of course, and music is playing. I walk in and everyone is smiling at me, giving me nods of joy.

"Everyone, I gathered you all together because Princess has something to say to you all," Draken says, commanding silence. He and his father exchange a nod, and his mother blows him a kiss. He turns and places a kiss on my forehead, and then he joins his brothers. Now they are all staring at me, shit. "You have the floor."

"Well, I, wow, you are all here. I would like to say thank you for saving me, for leaving your land to come and rescue me from that crazy dragon lady. I would like you all to know that I'm so grateful for each and every one of you." I turn and look at Beauka. "Thank you, Beauka, for coming. Also, Draken told me how you have never done anything like that before, and I would like you to know you are awesome, and I look forward to being your sister.

I'm going to need a girl to talk with among all these guys." I smile, and everyone is smiling, and then all this clapping starts and cheers and roars, Draken comes up and kisses my cheek.

"You are amazing, Princess. You know you didn't have to thank them. They promised to protect you and that is what they did. Your heart is so good, you gave Velca mercy when I would have killed her, you just made my sister feel great, and she is not easy. I love you, Princess."

"I love you too, Prince Draken," I say, laughing.

"Oh, so now you call me Prince Draken, no, I'm always just Draken to you, never your prince. Even in the future when I'm king, I'm Draken to you," he says, making me warm and causing me to feel butterflies again. We need to get back to my family so we can start this wedding planning, as I'm sure my mother is going out of her mind trying to come up with ideas.

"Draken, we need to go back, so I can start planning the wedding with my other family," I say, gauging his response.

He takes a deep breath. "Yes, we do, I will arrange for us to leave this evening. Do you have a day in mind?"

"Well it's June 10th today. My mom will need a month, so July 11th, is that okay?" I say, blushing. I'm not sure why I'm even blushing, maybe it's Draken and his sexiness.

"Yes that will be perfect, Princess; your eyes will change back to brown when we get back to earth. I don't like that, but I will get over it. I know this means a lot to you. Let's go get ready. My brothers will prepare for the portal for you," he says. "After I inform the family of going back to earth to prepare for the wedding, we will return for our ceremony here." I can't wait to see D. I miss him so much.

DRAKEN

I wish two weddings were not necessary, but I will adjust.
Showken, Layern and Hawken will come with us right now, and
the others will join us closer to the wedding. I look at Princess as
we sit in the garden, waiting for Showken and Hawken to show up.
Layern is already with us. Finally, they come walking up.

"What the hell took so long?" I ask, a little annoyed to be
going back to Earth. I glance at Princess. She looks nervous.

"Showken was the holdup. He was occupied with one of his
many friends," Hawken says, coming to stand by me.

"Hey, I'm on time, kind of. Okay, Cess, you're going to have
to use your ring, it will protect you."

"I don't know how," Princess says.

"Princess, just cover yourself like you did during the fighting, and it will be easier for you," I say, a little confused. How did she do it last time?

"I don't know how it happened. I asked for help and started crying, and then it opened up. I don't know how to do it again."

"Okay, look at your ring and command it to shield you," I say, taking her hand.

"Draken, you do it, you should know how to do this. I'm new to all of this," she says. Showken comes up, taps my shoulder and says, "Do it, Draken, and teach her later." She looks sexy; I'm taking her to bed when we get there.

"Okay, Princess, close your eyes." She does, placing her hands down by her side. I command the ring to cover her and it opens, giving her a covering.

"Okay, open them back up," I say. Her hands go to the cover, and I touch her hand.

"I'm opening the portal, Cess. Hang on," Showken says, laughing. He opens the portal and we are off, moving at a great speed, and Princess' eyes are closed or so I thought. She sees the man and dragon of me coming through the portal. It's what happens. We are back in Paradise Valley, Arizona. We all come through the portal in the study in our home. I wave my hand to remove the covering, and see her eyes are their birth color again. It saddens me to see her without my mark, but she runs to me and places her hands around my waist.

"We have to get to my parents, and start this planning."

"Yes, we do. But not before I take you to bed," I say, as she blushes.

"Draken!"

"Umm, can you both go to the room when you're going to have sex talk," Showken says, getting comfortable on the sofa. I drag Princess to the room and we continue there, which leads us to the bed, naked. That is exactly what I wanted.

***

"Mother, you are not inviting the entire country club," Princess says. I'm having a conversation with her father about doing business together. I smile, as Princess' mother is having a good time. I can see that her friends are happy for her, too. Kelly is still upset about Showken, I can tell, but her other friends are just thrilled about it all.

"Princess, you only get married once, and I want this to be the best event for you, so please let me have this, you're my only daughter," her mother says, she's gotten her way. Princess smiles.

"Okay, Mother."

The wedding plans continue every day. From choosing colors to flowers, tuxedos, food, music and even the place is debated some, but the day finally comes and all of my brothers have arrived for this day. Beauka didn't come, as she really hates the portal. She will make up for it at our ceremony in our land, Princess' new home.

"It's time, brother, let's go so you can marry Cess on Earth," Showken says, handing me the jacket to my tuxedo.

"Yes, let's go. I can't wait to see her," I say, as we head out. She made her brother the best man. I didn't argue. I know how much she loves him and how much she will miss him. I will make sure she gets back when it's possible, so she can see him. We are in a partially enclosed and partially outside space. We decided on an early wedding, as the heat is too much for the humans. It's only 9:00 a.m. D and my brothers walk out, and I hear many women's gasps. I chuckle, because Showken is going to find someone for each of my brothers, maybe even D. He seems to hold his own when finding a girl. The music starts playing and bridesmaids start walking down the aisle. They look lovely, but I can't wait to see Princess. The music changes and she is at the end with her father. I swallow, she looks amazing. I can't wait to have her in my arms. The décor looks great. I see my Princess, and I'm captivated by her beauty. Her dress is white and really pretty. I preferred her in purple, but I think her mother would have had a heart attack. She starts down the long walk, and everyone is standing. I feel my beast growling, and send her the growl. I see her smile as she accepts my heat. I truly love this woman.

"She looks beautiful," D says to me.

"I couldn't agree more." She finally reaches me, and the

ceremony begins. I go through the earthly ceremony. I hear "you may kiss the bride," and dive right in, forgetting the people and possessing her mouth in front of everyone. We turn, and are presented as Mr. and Mrs. Draken Draglen. Everyone claps, and we walk down the aisle, as we will now be taking pictures.

***

It is now our reception and everyone is greeting us. Every man that tries to hug Princess is given a growl, but I tolerate the handshakes. They have some crazy idea of dancing with the bride, I shot that off the program. I could not contain my beast with so many hands on her. Then it was time for me to get her garter off. I'm a little uncomfortable with this as well, but I go with it, as it's I who touch her. She sits in a chair in front of me and I get down on my knees, this could be fun.

"Princess, you look really pretty, but I like it when you blush, so-" I say. Her back is to the crowd of single men, and I'm going up her dress and her face is getting flushed.

"Draken, please."

"Please, what?" I say, chuckling. I finally see her garter, which I was told would be blue, because of the tradition. I look up at her and she is smiling. I can't help but lean forward and kiss her. I hear shouts of "you have to wait till later". Fuck them, I want a kiss right now.

"Thank you," I say, removing the garter from her leg, getting in good squeezes as I pull down the very purple garter. I hear the howling and I see all my brothers are standing, but none of them would dare to try to catch it.

"You're welcome, husband," I love the sound as it rolls off her lips. I turn and see D. I glance at Layern, who is close, and when I throw it, Layern makes sure D catches it. Everyone was yelling and laughing. After my Princess throws her flowers and Donna Marie catches them, we leave in a car to catch a plane that is waiting for us.

"I finally have you to myself," I say, reaching for her and pulling her into my lap. "You look amazing."

"You look amazing. My aunts, cousins and friends all want you. They all say you are a good catch," she says, laughing.

"Well, Princess, where would you like to go? I will take you anywhere in the world so we can have a honeymoon," I say, smiling. I miss my land, but I will give her what she wants without complaint.

"I would like to . . . go home," she says, biting her lip. I look at her, making sure of what I heard.

"Say that again." I have to hear it again.

"I want to go home, Draken. I've seen many places here on earth, my new home is a place I've yet to explore. So, I thought we could go to a romantic place in, umm, Cortamagen." She smiles, proud that she said it right, and so am I.

"Home we shall go. I will have the plane dismissed and I will take over driving, but I must get you out of this dress. One, you look really good and two, my mother would freak to see you in white, which is another color for another brother," I say, as she frowns, not understanding. I'll explain it later.

"Okay, Draken, I'm happy to be yours officially, and now I'm part of the family," she says, as I continue to undress her in the back seat. I will portal us out after I have my way with her in the back seat of this really large limousine.

"Oh, well I'm glad that you are glad to be with me, now let's get happy and get naked," I growl, and she rips my shirt open. Yes, Princess, all of this is yours, do what you want.

CESS

We arrive back home, but not in Draken's bedroom. We're standing near a waterfall, and the scenery is unreal. Draken smiles.

"I thought before we go back to the castle to get ready for another ceremony, we could have some alone time. Your mother never sleeps and always wanted your time, we never made love except a couple of times the entire time there, and that includes the car. So I thought we would make up for lost time. My family will prepare everything for us, so we can stay here for about a week or two, if you want," he says, giving me the sexiest look ever. I'm nervous about being in the woods without things I'm used to.

"I feel your reservations, Princess. It is stocked with food, and someone will come and restock every few days. I think you will like the cabin and yes, we have a bathroom, but I would like to get into my private lake, which is now yours as well. The temperature will be perfect, and it has tons of places that I can sit so you can ride me."

"Well, show me your cabin then," I smile, gesturing to him to lead the way.

"No, Princess, walk with me, and it's your cabin, too," he says, walking me to the door. He bends and picks me up.

"Draken!" I squeal.

"I thought that was what earthly men did, carry their wives over the threshold." He laughs, walking in and placing me on my feet. Shit, this is not a cabin, it's jewels, food, flowers and music playing. A huge bed is in the middle of the room, with piles of firewood on the floor in front of the bed. I've never seen that before, guess it's what they do in this land. I see desserts and strawberry cake. I love it. If this is what he calls a cabin, and I'm sure it's more like a 6 star hotel suite, I will cabin with him any day.

"Thank you for everything, it's beautiful and yes, I would love to spend some quality time alone with you," I say.

"And my beast, I want you not to be afraid of him, and out here I can change and you can get more acquainted with him, Princess," he says, pulling me close.

"I would love that, Draken, now what are . . . oh." He starts taking off my shirt and removing my other clothes, not saying a word. He steps back to remove his, and I grab his hand.

"I want to, please?" I ask, pouting a little.

"You don't ever have to ask, Princess, I'm all yours," he says, stepping forward and crowding me. He is so good at seduction. I'm going to have to learn this. I'm not as gentle and patient. I rip his shirt open, and get more excited as I unbutton his pants. I'm going to pleasure him this time. I want him to scream out. Well, at least try. I finally get his pants unzipped, and I hear him growl when I release him. I pull his pants off. I begin giving him gentle kisses on his chest, moving slowly down his body. I make my way to his knees, and see him looking at me.

"I'm so glad your eyes are back. You're mine, beautiful."

"Yes, I am," I say, and start planting small wet kisses on his erection. I feel it jump in my hands. It's so hot, but it doesn't burn. I take one long lick across its head, and the growl is loud.

"Princess, I can't take it," he says, eyes glowing purple. I smile, as I'm achieving what I want.

"Yes, you can," I say, taking him in my mouth. Oh, he tastes good. I have been waiting to please him. I squeeze my mouth tight and begin sliding him in and out of my mouth. He is so huge that I can't get him all the way in, but I will get as much as possible. I feel his hand in my hair, and his body moving to the rhythm of my mouth.

"GRRRR, Princess! You're killing me!" He growls before I can get going really well, I'm off my feet and on the bed, with my legs around his neck. He slides in easily. I'm wet right now from having him finally in my mouth. Mmmm, I have to work on his tolerance, though.

"Princess, you made me very happy, now hold on," he says, and goes to work on me as he is thrusting in and out of me. He takes no mercy on my breasts, sucking, biting, and pulling on my nipples.

"Draken," I whisper, as he starts with that slow pace in a circle, twisting and turning inside me.

"Louder, Princess." I whimper, as I can't find my voice; he has my mind in the clouds. "Princess, let me hear it now."

"DRAAAAKEN!" I yell, and he picks up the pace, taking us both over the edge. He pulls me close and starts singing to me again in his language. It's so beautiful the tears are rolling down my cheek. I truly love this man.

***

The day of the ceremony has come quickly. I'm nervous because I don't know what to expect. I'm with his mother and sister as I get ready. I'm wearing a beautiful, very light purple dress, that is not like any wedding dress I've ever seen. The split is in the middle, and rises all the way to the middle of my thighs. My cleavage is extremely low, and I don't have on shoes. My hair is down and my makeup is very little. I don't ask questions, as his mother and

Beauka sing praises of how beautiful I look. The jewelry is exquisite. I'm wearing, I know, millions of dollars worth of jewels. They are all purple and gold jewels, with small diamonds. The purple ones are a jewel only made in this land. I found that out from Beauka. I will be the only one ever to wear this color of jewels and clothing. What an honor.

"It's time, Cess," his mother says. "Beauka and I will leave now. You will come alone, and Draken will guide you to the place."

"What? I have to find my own way to the ceremony?" I say, panicking. What kind of wedding is this? I don't want to be left alone.

"Cess, you are not alone, as soon as you step out the door my son will be with you, guiding you to the main garden. It's a way to show the connection between you and Draken, as you come closer you will be able to find your way. Don't worry, my son knows where you are and is watching. Fear should not be your emotion, only joy." She leans over and gives me a kiss, Beauka gives me a kiss and they walk out of the room. Okay, so when I'm ready, I walk out of the room to be told by Draken, in my head, where to go. I should have asked more questions about this. I feel like I need to pee again. I begin to take some deep breaths. I've already married him. This is another ceremony to get through, then I will be done with all of this ceremony stuff. Well, here goes. I open the door and step out into the hall, and I feel him instantly.

"Hello, Princess, follow my voice," he says, and for some reason I know what to do. I turn right and begin my walk. I feel his heat and love, all at once. It's so strong it makes me weak. "I love you, Princess, and I vow to love you always."

"I vow to love you too, Draken."

"You are the beat of my soul, Princess, and I need you more than I can ever want you," he says, and I turn left. I'm so overcome with emotion that I can't speak.

"This is your castle, your home, your land, your people," he says, and I feel the need to touch the walls. "You will want for nothing, and I give myself to you always." I stop walking, as his words are so much. "Keep coming, Princess. Everyone wants to meet you, the Key to the land," he says, and I let his voice pull me and now I can feel him more, I must be close. I want to run to him, but I walk.

"Draken, I love you so much." I'm crying. This way of marrying is more emotional. The tears are flowing.

"Whenever you need me, remember I'm always near, holding you, guiding you, forever. I will never leave you. I will always kill for you, and I will die for you," he says, and I reach a huge archway with thousands of people. It could be millions, I'm not sure, but this garden doesn't have an end. Flowers are everywhere and the people are standing. I'm getting nervous as to what to do.

"Come forward and let the people see you, Princess." I walk and I look down, and my dress is darkening from the very light purple to a deep purple. I walk out and the people are staring. I thought Draken would be waiting for me. I feel his presence even more, and I turn and he is walking toward me in a fine, purple silk shirt, but it's very thin, and purple pants. A sigh of relief comes over me as he reaches me. I notice that the closer he comes, the more our purples come together to the same shade. The tears continue to flow, this is beautiful. He finally reaches me and places a kiss on my cheek, wiping my tears away.

"I love you, Draken,"

"I love you more, Princess." He turns me and there are huge steps that we must walk up, I'm sure, as all his brothers are there in the colors of their dragons. I take the walk with him as he holds my hand. We reach the top, and the crowd is very quiet. I hope they like me.

"I love your legs, Princess," Draken says. "Are you ready?"

"Yes, who performs the ceremony?" I ask, seeing no one coming forth.

"I do, my wella, trust me," he says. I nod, and he takes a step back from me.

"Close your eyes and I will give myself over to you, and take you as you take me," he says, and that sounds like something I don't want to happen in front of everyone.

"Draken, what-"

"Trust me?"

"Yes, I do," I say, watching his eyes turn a deep purple. I close my eyes.

"Keep them closed, and I will tell you when to open."

"Okay," he says. I start to feel warm all over, and the heat is growing through my body, yet it feels so good. I almost want to moan. I can feel it everywhere, even in my mouth, even my hair feels hot. And then I smell Draken all around me, and it feels like he is kissing my body all at once, not missing a spot.

"Open, my Wella," he says. I open my eyes and my entire body is engulfed in a purple flame. I'm on fire, but not burning. I actually feel really good and warm. I want to have sex with him right now.

He turns me towards the crowd and says, "People, met Princess Frances Draglen, Wella to Prince Draken Draglen, and heir to the throne of Cortamagen." The crowd erupts into a cheer so loud that I'm still on fire, and yet I'm not scared and I don't even have to pee. This feels right; this is my home, my land, and my husband. Draken holds me and we kiss, and the flame surrounds us both and everyone is on their feet dancing and throwing flowers at us. I'm so into the kiss I don't realize the fire is gone. His brothers are clapping. His mother is in tears, and his father blows me a kiss which I catch, and Draken raises a eyebrow at his father. I laugh because I don't think he will ever get over his jealousy.

"Beautiful hair," he says, touching it and bringing it to his nose. I notice that it's jet black, like his hair. Oh my, I'm truly his, really.

"Come, they will party, we will go fly," he says, and no fear enters me, just excitement. I'm going to fly with my Draken. He leads me to the center of the garden and changes into the dragon. I don't need help getting on. I climb him as he dips his head for me. I see why the split in the dress needed to be so long, I hold on to Draken and he takes off and we fly away and I see them recede into the distance, everyone waving and smiling and the party going on.

***

We are on a cliff extremely high in the sky now. Draken is in human form, and we have made love twice already. I love him and I love his dragon.

"Well, were you happy with the ceremony? Just a little different from your wedding."

"Yes just a little different, but I loved it. It was so beautiful, Draken," I say, curling up under him even more.

"So, Princess, we need some Youngs," he says, smiling.

"Youngs? Draken, are you talking about children?" I ask, smiling. I was afraid of carrying his child, but now I'm excited.

"Yes, Youngs, and I think we should start on our honeymoon."

"Are we having another one?" I ask, giggling.

"Why, yes, Princess, we need to get started on my heirs," he says, rolling me over on my back, and showering me with kisses. I'm so happy to be with Draken forever. I never thought this would be how my life would turn out, that I would live in another realm with my dragon man.

"Will you still have to run the business and leave me?" I ask, not wanting to see him leave for months at a time.

"No, Showken will run the business, in fact he leaves to go back in a few months. No more talking, Princess, we need to practice for those Youngs."

I smile and fall even more in love with him, as Draken and I fall into an abyss of our love together.

Thank you for taking the time to read DRAKEN, the first book in the Draglen Brothers series.

Please enjoy the first chapter of the next book, "SHOWKEN."

SHOWKEN

Why the hell did Draken choose me to run the business? Damn. If I'm running it, then human women are allowed in the car, house, and definitely the office. I'm happy Layern and Hawken are coming along. Gemi decides to stay, but Domlen decided he would come, also.

"Okay, I'm in charge now and I say there are no rules, except don't expose us or I will be fucking pissed," I say. Layern ignores me. Hawken and Domlen just look.

"You're not running shit," Hawken says.

"I run everything," I say, "and unlike Draken, I will burn your ass, and that will take months to heal. Now, who's up for a drink at a bar I've been dying to go to?"

"I'm up for it. What's the name of the bar?" Domlen says, not looking up from his laptop.

"Hot Chicks and Drinks," Layern says, looking serious. I have to make sure Layern gets laid. Domlen and Hawken and I have nothing to worry about.

"Well lets go see what's in the Hot Chicks and Drinks Bar. I think this might be my lucky day."

I go to my room to get ready. I love human women, and plan on bringing at least two home tonight. I just don't like when they get all "Showken, you going to call," or "Showken, I think I love you," to hell with that. I don't want that shit. I just want a good lay, and to keep it moving. I may settle down in about, oh, another hundred years, but right now I'm having fun. I walk back, Domlen and Layern are ready. Hawken didn't bother to change.

"Okay, no hurting the human women. If they say no, respect it and move on. Don't start any fights, as we have to go to work on Monday. Please, don't fall in love like Draken, he went crazy. Now he is hooked on Cess. I don't have time for a repeat." I grab the keys to the Hummer.

"Showken, stop giving out orders, you sound like Draken. He always wants to give out orders," Hawken says. We all laugh.

"Yeah, but now Cess is giving the orders," Domlen says. Layern shakes his head.

"Let's just go have some fun. Look, we're already here,"

Hawken says.

We all walk into the bar, and it's pretty packed, but its Friday. I'm casing the place, and see her behind the bar placing drinks on a tray. She has dark brown hair, hanging straight. Her body has all the right curves. Yes, she is going to be one of them tonight. She looks mad, but I'll just smile. She will melt and the panties will be off.

"I'm going to get a waitress for us, go find a table," I say, heading straight for her.

"Stop giving out orders!" Hawken yells out. I ignore his jealous ass and keep moving until I'm right in front of her.

"Excuse me. My brothers and I need our order to be taken," I say, hoping she will look up. Instead, she keeps placing drinks on the tray to deliver.

"So fucking what. Wait your turn," she says, and moves around me, walking toward another table. Shit. This one has some issues. It doesn't matter. I still want to have her in my bed tonight. I walk to our table, and sit. She walks over with a small pad and pen.

"What can I get you boys?"

"Boys?" Domlen says, "You see any boys?"

"As a matter of fact, yes. Now what you want to drink?"

Oh, she is really angry. I like it.

"We would like some pitchers of beer, the best you have," Layern says.

"Is that all?" She asks, not looking at any of us. I wonder what that's all about. She can't be shy with a mouth like that. Hmmm . . .

"Yes, I would like to know what time you're off?" I ask, trying to get her to look at me. She finally does. There are those beautiful grey eyes. She is one angry lady, but I like her. She could be fun.

"Look, I'm not interested. I'll be back with the beer," she says, walking away. I watch her sexy walk, back to the bar counter to get our orders. She is a woman. Her ass, breasts, and hips are perfect.

"Showken, I think you should leave this one alone. She is very good at blocking emotion, but I was able to sense that she is very angry and damaged," Layern says.

"I think you guys can talk about this, I've spotted my fun for tonight," Hawken says, heading over to a table with a couple of ladies. They look fun, all smiles, but I want her. She basically said 'fuck off' to me, and that is not happening.

"She's an angry human female, but she is not allowed to call me boy again, or she'll-" Domlen says, just as our pitchers arrive. She sets them down, and I slide a hundred towards her.

"Here's your beer, and is this to start a tab?" she snaps.

"Nope, it's your tip for being so nice," I say, giving her a wicked smile. She is angry, huh? Well, I will see if she is really not into me, or just too scared to admit it. I notice she just stares at me, and we do this staring thing for a good ten seconds before she blinks.

"I'll start your tab," she says, snatching the money and walking away.

"I see that Hawken is having a good time, I'm going to claim myself some fun, too." Domlen says, pouring himself a glass and taking a pitcher with him, heading towards Hawken and the women.

"Layern, what is it about her?" I ask, not taking my eyes off her as she takes orders and delivers them.

"You shouldn't, but since she gave you a challenge, I see you will stop at nothing to have her, just be careful," Layern takes a long gulp. "I'm going to dance and have some fun, too. I think you should come too. I see those women on the floor dancing our way, they are waiting for us," he says, rising, and moving closer to the dancing floor, which is not very big, but big enough.

"I'll join you in a second, get them warm and I'll be over to relieve you of one," I say, smiling, knowing Layern is good at dancing. He can handle two or three human women at once. Layern walks away shaking his head. I continue staring at her. I need her name. I walk to the bar, blocking her from going behind it.

"What the hell you doing?" she yells at me, trying to go around. I just smile, and wait for her to look at me. Finally her head rises to meet mine. She is beautiful, even angry.

"What's your name?"

"I'm not telling you my name. You're more than likely a stalker as you can't take a hint already," she snaps, placing her hands on those lovely hips. "Now move!" She looks me dead in my eyes, but I see a guard up, not anger. Huh, I need to know more.

"I'm Showken. You are . . ." I say, raising a brow. She is not getting past without a name.

"Marilyn, now can you move?" she says through her teeth.

"That wasn't hard, Marilyn, and yes, I will move, for now," I say, stepping aside and making sure to feel her heat as she slides past me, trying not to touch. I stand and listen as she gives the bartender her order for another table. She looks pissed, but I still want her. She just has to be difficult, and I love a challenge. She turns and looks at me, rolling her beautiful eyes. Oh, yes, this one I will have. I return a wide smile, and head for the dance floor. I pull the first girl I see out of her seat, and dance with her seductively. The lady is very willing and aroused, but my eye is on Marilyn as she watches the show. I sniff the air, and there it is; she is hot. She likes my dancing. I make eye contact with her, then we just stare at each other, and I mouth "I want you," licking my lips for her pleasure. I really need this woman. I see Domlen and Hawken walk out with their fun for tonight. Smiling, I nod to them. The song ends, and Layern meets me at the table.

"Showken, what is it about her? I'm picking up anger and

arousal, but the anger is way more intense. The human you were just dancing with is willing to do whatever with you," Layern says, drinking straight from the only pitcher left. I smile, knowing she has to come back.

"Marilyn!" I yell, forcing her to look again. She looks sexy as hell walking this way. I may just want her because she said no. Whatever the reason, I can't help but rise to the challenge. Finally getting to our table, she places her hands on her hips, narrowing beautiful grey eyes at me.

"We need more pitchers," I say, raising my brow and sliding another hundred dollar bill her way. She snatches again, and storms off without a word. She says nothing, heading for the bar.

"You are really pissing her off," Layern says, finishing the pitcher.

"I know, that's the point. She's very angry, very hot, too. I think a little fun will help her out," I say, not taking my eyes off her as she brings four pitchers back to the table. I wonder does she think she can get me drunk? She bangs them down, spilling some, and storms off angrily. I tilt my head, watching her walk away is amazing.

"Layern, I'm not giving up on this one. After I have my fun I'll leave her alone," I say, grabbing a pitcher, and taking a huge gulp.

"Ok, but I'm telling you, this one is not for fun. She has secrets that I can't get to. I'd stay clear if I were you, but seeing the sparkle in your eye, brother, I know you will stop at nothing. So good luck."

"Luck? Shit, I plan on having a good time with Ms Marilyn," I say. "Her anger only excites me. Besides, I don't think she knows how angry I can get." I watch her maneuver through the crowd delivering beers.

She ignores me for the rest of the night. Layern invites some ladies to the table, and they are very willing, but I can't keep my eyes off her. I give attention to the redhead purring next to me, but I don't want an easy lay tonight. I want a challenge, and I see I have one. Studying her walk, how she stands, her eyes, I smile, thinking it will be fun getting to know her. She shakes her head every time she looks my way, sighing in frustration. Yes, I'm in her mind, now I want in that body of hers.

"I'm going home, brother. You coming?" Layern says, standing with a lady on his arm. I stare at him in confusion, I know who already holds my brother's heart. Maybe he's over her.

"I think I'll make sure Marilyn gets home safe, but you have some fun with both," I say, leaning over and giving the redhead next to me a kiss. "Sweetheart, you and your friend will take care of my brother, right?" I smile, and she melts.

"Yes, of course," she says, rising. Layern takes her arm, and they all go for the door. It's getting late. I will stay until she leaves.

I need to see what I'm up against.

I hope you have enjoyed reading DRAKEN and the first chapter of the next book, SHOWKEN!

SHOWKEN will be out by the end of October 2013.

Solease M Barner

Book 2 in the Draglen Brothers series

SHOWIEN

THE DRAGLEN BROTHERS SERIES

Solease M Barner

Book 3 in the Draglen Brothers series

LAYERN

THE DRAGLEN BROTHERS SERIES

Contact

I love to connect with readers! Here is where you can find me.

https://www.facebook.com/TheDrakenBrothersASeriesBySoleaseMBarner

https://www.facebook.com/solease.marksbarner

Other books by this Author

If you are interested in more works by Solease M Barner, checkout
https://www.facebook.com/TheSecretsOfTheGhostsTrilogy
"Secrets of the Ghosts-The Sleeper"
"Secrets of the Ghosts-AWAKENS"

COMING SOON!
"Secrets of the Ghosts-REDEMPTION"
Amazon - http://www.amazon.com/Solease.-M-
Barner/e/B008N3FVGY/ref=sr_ntt_srch_lnk_1?qid=1379470656
&sr=1-1

SOLEASE M BARNER

SECRETS

OF THE

GHOSTS

THE SLEEPER

SOLEASE M BARNER

SECRETS

OF THE

GHOSTS

BOOK 2

AWAKENS

Solease M Barner

SECRETS

OF THE

GHOSTS

REDEMPTION

Book 3

About the Author

Solease lives in a quiet area. She is a wife, and mother to a daughter. Solease loves to spend time with her family. She's been called the social butterfly by many friends. She's a huge movie buff, and loves to read books. She writes poetry on a daily basis, as a way to release stress. Solease is the author of "Secrets of the Ghosts - The Sleeper", "Secrets of the Ghosts - AWAKENS", and "The Draglen Brothers Series - DRAKEN"

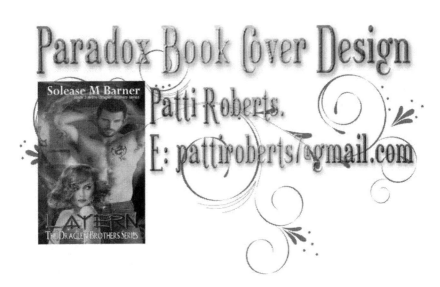

Paradox Book Cover Design
Patti Roberts.
E: pattiroberts7@gmail.com

Solease M Barner

LAYERN
The Draglen Brothers Series

http://paradoxbooktrailerproductions.blogspot.com.au/

Made in the USA
Columbia, SC
04 October 2018